BEACH MEMORIES

BEACH HOUSE ROMANCE
BOOK 2

JULIE CAROBINI

DOLPHIN GATE BOOKS

Beach Memories (Beach House Romance, Book 2)

JULIE CAROBINI writes sweet beach romances from her home on the California coast. Please visit her at JulieCarobini.com.

ONCE UPON A TIME ...

I wrote a series about five siblings who inherited a beach house—with a catch!

That was in 2020 ... and we all know what happened *that* year. Life was turbulent so I decided to do something different: I released all five books under a pen name.

But ... I found it difficult to maintain two personas. I also wanted to add a bit more content to these stories. So I pulled the novels from publication, added new scenes, and re-covered the series under my own name.

If you like tropes, such as fake relationships, billionaires, secret babies, and cowboys, then I know you'll love the revised and refreshed Beach House Romance series!

Now, turn the page for book two ...

Julie

1

"We're depending on you, Jake."

Jake slammed his truck door and stepped quickly across the parking lot of the Clothing Mart, his sister's admonition ringing in his mind. Maggie was the eldest—and bossiest—of his four sisters, and though he was older than her by nearly two years, she still had a way of making him listen.

He chuckled, despite the predicament he found himself in—the same predicament all his siblings found themselves in: Jake and his sisters had inherited their parents' beach house.

Some might have found that enviable, but he found the circumstances ... odd. After their parents' untimely deaths, he and his siblings discovered their mother and father's assets had been given away to various charitable causes. Except for their summer home—their well-worn, in-need-of-work beach house.

The catch? Each sibling had to live in the house for a full

month and make necessary repairs. And they had to do so on a strict budget. If they refused, the house would be given away to charity. No exceptions. At the end of the five months, the executor of their parents' estate informed them, they had to decide together what would be done with the house. He shuddered. Being the lone brother to four sisters, this didn't bode well for him.

A cheery man in a blue vest greeted him. "May I direct you, sir?"

"Men's clothing."

The elderly man smiled kindly and gestured toward the farthest corner of the warehouse-sized structure. *Of course.* Jake offered his thanks and snaked his way through the store's overcrowded aisles.

"You're not in the big city anymore," Maggie had chided him earlier on the phone. "So get yourself some clothing suitable for the beach—get rid of those wing tips you wear to business meetings and please start work on our parents' house right away. We need to sell it soon!"

There had been an urgency in Maggie's voice. He had noticed that same tone for quite some time really—not just on this call. After a few well-placed calls of his own, Jake learned that his big sister was having some financial problems. And he'd taken steps to help her, though no one in his family knew what he was up to—that was strictly between him and his banker.

Jake blew out a breath, clearing his mind the best he could. In addition to family troubles, tiresome accusations and a mammoth lawsuit awaited him in Los Angeles where he lived and worked nonstop. Like Maggie, he wanted nothing more than to serve his month-long sentence at the beach house and make the improvements necessary for him and his sisters to get top dollar for it—then let it go.

A wall of denim greeted him. He exhaled. Not the brands he was used to, but they would do. He grabbed three folded pairs in his size and stacked them in his arms. Next, he moved to a table of board shorts and T-shirts in vibrant colors. Neon ... everywhere. No thanks.

He added a couple of pairs of shorts to his stack and scanned overhead signs for directions to plain, white undershirts. There. He made a beeline for the next section where a ladder partially obscured the wall of white cotton tees.

That's when he spotted her: a woman standing on the highest rung of the rolling staircase, her feet shod in stilettos, her skirt short enough to call him to task for noticing. He glanced around. Didn't this violate some kind of OSHA law?

He cleared his throat.

She stood at the top of the stairs, her gaze drifting lazily down its length. With one delicate hand curving around the railing, she seemed lost in thought. But when her eyes met his, something flickered on her face. It was a look that speared him, as if she held him in contempt.

As he looked closer, he couldn't help but notice the precarious position of her pointy heel hovering dangerously over the waffle-patterned step. Clearly, she was tottering and he wondered: What were the chances of that stiletto-heel landing solidly in one of those perfectly-sized holes?

"Can I help you down?" he asked, ignoring the dagger in her gaze.

Waves of blonde locks cascaded down her shoulders. She smirked. "No thanks. I've got it under control."

He crossed his arms. "I see that." A part of him

demanded that he walk away. Why would he choose to pick a fight with a stranger? And yet ... something in her expression egged him on. He pointed to a sign above the ladder that said Employees Only.

She snapped a smug smile at him, as if he were a naughty child. "How do you know I'm not an employee?"

"The absence of a brightly colored vest."

She nodded, though it was anything but sincere. "Right."

The woman turned her back on him and continued to hunt for whatever it was she was hunting for. Jake frowned. What in the world was her problem? He should walk away. Having sisters had taught him that. But ... but ... didn't she know how dangerous this was?

A male voice shouted from behind. "Excuse me, excuse me! I'm the manager here. What are you doing?"

The woman hurriedly pulled several more packages from shelves, kicked off her heels, and hopped down to the floor just as the manager reached them.

"You should have called for assistance," the guy said, scolding them both.

The woman paid no attention to him. Instead, she flashed Jake a rather victorious smile and handed him a package of wife-beater tank tops. "Here's what you were looking for, hon," she said sweetly.

Then, she disappeared.

DAISY RAN ALONG THE BEACH, the salty sea air filling her lungs. She pumped her arms to pick up speed, increasing the intensity, her feet sprinting through the sand. Colibri

Beach was not on her list of planned destinations at this point in her life. She had saved enough money from her job at Sly's Hardware all during high school to support herself into adulthood, and she had yet to dip into the small trust fund her father had left her.

After graduation, Daisy extended her wings, flying off with a charity relief organization, using her skills to build houses in Mexico and Belize, and to help repair them in hurricane-ravaged areas of the United States. She had pretty much mapped out her life, never considering that her mother might need her here—at least, not so soon.

She slowed, frustration filling her mind. Of all the times that she had to be here, Jake Morelli was home. How was that for bad luck? Guilt twisted her insides because, truthfully, she shouldn't be complaining. If it hadn't been for Jake's sister, Grace ...

She didn't want to think about *what-ifs*. Her childhood home had been badly burned and, thankfully, Grace had found her mother before it was too late.

With this sudden turn of events in her mother's life, Daisy had taken time off from her work to hopefully fix the drafty old house she'd always known. She released a sigh into the wind. Her mother had always wanted a girly girl, but instead, she got her—a girl who liked to get out of bed in the morning and run outside, shoes off, hair flying, ready to dig up sand crabs before all the sandpipers got 'em. A girl who spent most of her growing-up years with smudges on her face and freckles earned from the sun.

She groaned, running faster. A seagull dive-bombed her and Daisy shook her fist at the cranky bird. *Just you wait!*

Really, though, was this going to be all that hard? Surely

she would find someone to take over care of her mother
once she made the place livable again. Her mother was an
independent woman. No way would Daisy attempt to deny
her the right to her own home, though that annoying realtor,
Lillian Madsen, would like nothing better than to acquire
the listing.

No. Positively, no.

Wren Mcafee would be staying in her home, surrounded
by its beautiful lavender bushes, until her last breath. Daisy,
her daughter, would make the necessary repairs and then
move on. And that would be that.

Still, she couldn't get the face of that annoying Jake out of
her mind. Why did he have to show up here? Oh, she knew
about his parents' strange Last Will and Testament, but any
one of the Holloway siblings could have been here this
month. Why him now? And of all the weirdest of places to
run into him—Clothing Mart. He acted as if he had never
seen her before. *Typical.* They had only known each other
for years—though their paths had not crossed in many since
then—but whatever!

She was a stranger to him. And she preferred to keep it
that way. Made for a cleaner break.

Daisy clenched her teeth, remembering how cruel he
could be. Some people remembered the exact words that
haunted them. They could quote the things that others had
said that cut deeply, but Daisy struggled with those kinds of
recollections. Instead, she remembered how people and
experiences made her *feel*. And seeing Jake again brought
back all of those feelings of rejection again.

Then again, she'd had the last word yesterday, hadn't
she? A smile tickled her face. He'd stood there looking so

smug, waiting for her to fall off that stairway. Probably thought he would catch her like some swoon-y cowboy or something. Handing him wife beaters was a stroke of inspiration that she hadn't seen coming—but it worked. By the wide-eyed expression on his mug, she could tell that he hadn't expected her to walk away and leave him to deal with management.

She considered that a big win.

A flicker of sweat dropped from her chin. Always a sign of a good run. Even with the sea breeze, she'd worked up a sweat, something she needed right now. She had been taken aback by the work her mother's home needed. The fire damage to the exterior wall and her mother's subsequent recovery had reminded her just how fragile life could be. Again, she found herself thinking that if it weren't for Grace and that hunky husband of hers rushing to her mother's aid at just the right moment ... well, chills ran through her at the never-ending loop that kept spinning through her head.

Thankfully, she had learned from the fire department that her mother's occasional penchant for smoking cigars had nothing to do with the fire.

She slowed her pace but kept jogging, remembering how it felt to walk into her childhood home for the first time since the accident. She'd put her hands to her face as her heart twisted in her chest. Even without the recent incident, the house looked worn, the walls dingy and in need of some love.

So she'd started by opening the curtains, desperate for some of the beach's gorgeous natural light to flow inside the house, but the windows ... oh, the windows! They were covered in salt from the sea air and grime. Lots and lots of grime.

Guilt and sorrow see-sawed through her. The house was going to need more than construction rehabilitation—it needed hands-on, tender lovin' care.

A male voice broke into her strained thoughts. "No high heels today?"

Daisy blinked and slowed further. Jake? She had vaguely noticed someone running toward her but hadn't given it much thought. If she had realized it was him, she would have taken a detour, a complete u-turn back down the beach.

Instead, she stopped next to him, one hand reflexively finding her hip. "Did the T-shirts fit?"

He crossed his arms, a glint of competition in his eyes. "Touché."

She wanted to smack that smirk right off his grizzled face. Not one sign of recognition showed up in his eyes.

"Almost didn't recognize you without your red dress," he said.

She peered at him from beneath the bill of her baseball cap. "And yet, you did." Maybe she had been wrong about him. At least he knew her now. That was something.

He grinned, despite her comeback.

"What brings you here?" Daisy said, though she felt anything but neighborly toward the man, who, as a boy, pretty much ignored her. Not to mention that time he turned her down flat ...

He flashed a grin, his white teeth glinting in the morning sunlight. She'd heard through the grapevine that he was some bigwig architect-builder down south—probably paid a lot of money for those teeth. He pointed to a spot behind her. "Rehabbing my childhood home. It's down the beach some."

Wait. She dug that hand deeper into her side and frowned. He was telling her where he grew up? Why would he do that if ... if he knew her?

An amused smile played on Jake's face. He dropped his gaze. "Why that look again?"

She lifted her chin. "What look?"

"The scowl. Same one you shot at me, a stranger, at the Clothing Mart." He could hardly contain his laughter—she could tell. The laughter died, but his smile remained. "Was it something I said?"

She stepped toward him until the toes of their running shoes met. She rose up on her toes until her eyes hit his ... chin. So he was tall? *Whatever.* She stared him down. "You don't remember me, do you?"

His brows dipped. "If I'm not mistaken, I believe that's the reason for our conversation."

"What are you talking about?"

"I do remember you. I recognized you from your high-wire act at the store, offered you a pleasant hello, and so here we are ... conversing."

Oh, he was smooth. Daisy kept her gaze on his, though, not letting him get out of this quite yet. "Yesterday I was wearing heels and a dress. How is it that you recognized me out here with a hat and running clothes?"

He didn't reply right away. Instead, he held his chiseled body steady, arms across his chest, feet spread wide. Jake Holloway looked too perfect. Still, his symmetrical brows, the crest of deep brown hair flowing in the exact direction of the sea breeze, and that well-crafted whisper of a beard couldn't hide the fact that he had a splattering of freckles across his nose. Just like when they were kids.

"Well," he said finally, "I suppose it was your size."

"My ... *what?*"

He chuckled. "You are ... petite."

Oh. That. Daisy knew she was short, but it never stopped her from pursuing life at full speed. She just wore heels doing it. Like she had yesterday when she stopped at the store on her way to meet someone at a friend's wedding. One thing she hadn't realized, though, was that her lack of height could so easily identify her to someone who, apparently, had no idea that they had met before.

Daisy shook her head, slowly. "You really have no idea who I am, do you?"

"Should I?" His voice continued to hold that tinge of humor in it. Not in a particularly cruel way, but in a manner that told her she was simply entertainment to him.

Daisy rocked back on her heels, madder than a gull who'd found an empty McDonald's bag. "Jake Holloway, I grew up in the house next to yours! Saw you every summer and sometimes in those in-between months, too."

He ran his gaze over her, causing her face to warm, and something dawned in his eyes. He leaned in closer. "The munchkin?"

Daisy rolled her eyes but kept herself from stomping a foot, like a toddler. No one had called her that in nearly eight years, and she didn't relish hearing it now. "It's Daisy," she emphasized. "Daisy Mcafee."

Jake's giddy smile dimmed. He tilted his head, the recognition dawning across his face. "Mcafee? Are you—"

"I'm Wren's daughter."

2

A misshapen cloud hovered over Jake's head. Daisy hated him, apparently, though he had no recollection of anything he had done in the past to invite such wrath. Weren't teenage boys supposed to be clueless? His mind replayed the smorgasbord of reactions Daisy had offered him moments ago on this beach—a glare, an eye roll, crossed arms, and one haughty chin.

A dog appeared at his feet, a large name tag swinging from her collar. "Sally" panted heavily as sea water dripped from her fur. She dropped a stick of driftwood onto one of his Adidas running shoes and whined.

Jake chucked the doggy under her chin and laughed. "Ready to run?"

The dog sidled backward, egging him on.

Jake faked her out a few times, then pitched the stick high into the air, far enough for it to land in the tide. Sally tore after it, and from a distance, her owner caught his attention and waved.

Jake kept on moving, soaking up the perfect weather. At least he had that going for him today. The air was crisp and warm at Colibri Beach, cheery enough to make him ask himself, at least once, why he had so seldom returned over the years.

One reason was obvious: time. Jake worked long, treacherous hours using his skills and passion to create sustainable, mixed-use commercial developments throughout Los Angeles. Buyers wanted to see eco-conscious designs that were foundational—not just a building with solar panels stuck on the roof to make things look eco-friendly. He worked arduously on balance, on providing free-flowing projects that maximized light and space, yet contained strong structural support.

To his mind, the study and execution of a building of any size was both art and science. Not to mention sweat. There had been other reasons he'd stayed away, but why bring up bygones now?

His cell phone rang and, eager to do away with his memories, Jake answered the call without looking at the screen.

"It's Mike. Got a second?"

Being on a first-name basis with his lawyer had its perks. Although at the moment, he couldn't name one.

"I do," he said. "Shoot."

"It appears we are having a problem locating Billy Bask. My office has exhausted its resources in serving him with a notice of deposition."

Jake clenched his jaw. Figures the guy would run. Although he had not been able to prove it yet, he believed Billy, the foreman on the Carter Hotels project, knew exactly how his official plans changed without Jake knowing about it. That change pitched Jake headfirst into hot water.

He glanced out to the gurgling, churning sea. "Thoughts on what to do next?"

"We are not giving up, of course. With your permission, I'd like to hire a private investigator to dig him up."

"My permission because this will cost more money."

"Precisely. My guy is reasonable, but depending on the time it takes, there could be a considerable cost to the process."

There wasn't anything to think about. Bask had to be found. "Then do it."

With a click, his lawyer hung up to chase after fine print and fugitives, leaving Jake to ruminate on that lingering cloud. As far as he could tell, no one in the family knew about this glitch in Jake's otherwise ripple-less career—not even his sister Grace, who, as a lawyer herself, would surely jump at the chance to study up on what he'd gotten himself into. Or rather, what his once-illustrious client had dragged him into.

Jake sucked up an all-consuming breath and let it out again. There was much that his family did not know about him. He had held his thoughts and activities private for as long as he could remember and it never bothered him ... until now. Something about being here again made him feel closer to the sisters he rarely saw in person.

Steps away from the beach house now, he slowed to stop, allowing himself to stand back and take in the old beast. The stillness of the house, once lit up and filled with nonstop noise—a byproduct of having so many sisters around along with their summertime friends—unnerved him.

And just like that, the tide turned his emotions and he had never disliked the beach so much.

A movement to his left caught his attention. Daisy emerged from her mother's house and stepped out onto the south-facing deck, the one opposite his family's home. She had replaced the baseball cap with a cowboy hat and wore goggles around her neck. He watched as she put a bottle of something on the table and carried a sander to the other side of the deck. There was nothing timid about the way she moved. Maybe that was another reason he had recognized her earlier today, though he had thought it had more to do with her diminutive size.

Daisy thought him a jerk. She hadn't said so in words, but she certainly did with that flash of flame in her eyes when she drew herself up on her toes to face him. He pressed his lips together, considering Daisy's reaction to him. He tried to think of her situation in reverse. If someone from his childhood didn't recognize him, he doubted he would care.

Then again, maybe he wouldn't have noticed either.

He curled another look at her. She tossed her hat onto the table and put the goggles on. Then she cranked up the sander and began working on a portion of ancient deck railing. Odd. Damage to the Mcafee house happened on the other side. He wasn't around when the fire started but was here soon after for a time. He examined the place then and took in the aftermath, and quite frankly, had been surprised the house had survived as long as it had.

The first thing he noticed was the mismatched siding on the wall that had been torched. If he had to guess, the exterior wall was a patch job gone wrong. Wasn't for him to say, though. He hadn't been asked, and besides, he felt certain Wren's insurance company would step in and make sure that repairs were done correctly. The last thing he wanted to do was draw attention to the problems he noticed. Jake had learned that cities were built on red tape, and he wasn't about to be the one to inflict that kind of mess on the Mcafee family, no matter what he thought of Wren.

His call with his sister yesterday infiltrated his mind, Maggie's voice so clear and recognizable in his head that he almost thought she was walking the beach with him right now.

She'd implored him as he hurried through the parking lot of Clothing Mart. "Why don't you like Wren again?"

"I never said I don't like her."

"But you avoid her."

"Not interested in talking about this right now, Mags."

"Don't Mags me. That's what all of you do when you don't want to answer my inquiring mind."

"It's just not important."

Maggie groaned into the phone. "Fine. Whatever. I have to get back to work anyway. Our fridge won't fill itself."

He paused. "Is everything okay with you and Eva in that regard?"

"Yes, yes, of course." She tried to brush him off with her dismissive tone, as if his concern for her and his niece wasn't necessary. "Getting back to Wren, I really wish you'd level with me."

He stopped. This had gone on long enough. Why was he keeping this all to himself anyway? "Fine. I'll tell you, but you need to take a deep breath first."

"Um, all right."

"I think she and our father had a dalliance."

"A ... dalliance?"

"Yes."

"First of all, brother, nobody uses that word anymore. Have you been reading Jane Austen or something? Second, what makes you think that?"

He crossed his arms, remembering back. "To your first question, never. And to your second, I showed up here once, when Mom was ... ill." For some reason, neither he nor his siblings had been fully aware of the extent of their mother's loss of mental awareness. All this time later, they barely spoke of it. "Anyway, I could tell that I had interrupted something."

"Oh no. Don't you tell me you saw them naked. I can handle a lot, but not that. Oh no."

He frowned. "You are making me sorry I told you."

"Right." She exhaled. "Sorry."

"And no, there was no shedding of clothes. They both looked guilty, though. Like I had interrupted something." He paused. "I want nothing to do with her."

Maggie didn't answer him right away and he feared he had stirred something up that would be too difficult for his sister to handle. As a single mother, she had enough stress in her life. He waited and readied himself to console her through the impact of this revelation.

Finally, she spoke. "Jake, I'm only going to say this once: You have lost your mind."

He had expected tears ... not chastisement. Jake's shoulders tensed. He stopped abruptly, debating whether to end the call and march inside Clothing Mart to get what he needed.

But Maggie continued. "I doubt seriously that our aging father and that old woman had a 'dalliance.' It doesn't matter now anyway—leave secrets buried with the dead."

He winced at the comeuppance his sister delivered.

"And I beg you," Maggie said, "do not mention any of this crazy talk to our sisters. Grace will want to investigate, Lacy will bring it up every chance she gets, and Bella will probably cry nonstop. I, for one, am not interested in fielding all those reactions!"

As he stood on the beach, reliving that conversation with his sister, Jake sensed the sizzle of a hard stare on him. He blinked, the sun's rays blinding, and shaded his eyes with his hand. Daisy watched him from her deck, a silent sander in one hand. He swallowed. Caught.

Why had he allowed his mind to wander like that while he stood here staring in her direction?

Daisy pulled the goggles from her eyes and stepped close to the railing, and when she did, he couldn't help but notice the peek of bare midriff below her knotted T-shirt. He'd been around job sites his whole career and could not recall what another soul wore, at least at this moment. She cupped that delicate mouth of hers with her hand. "We're not sellin' it to you, in case you're wondering!"

Selling? Jake assumed she meant Wren's house. He trudged across the sand until he reached the deck, noting that he'd gained an especially great view of that midriff now …

"Eyes up here," she said.

"Don't mind me. I'm just admiring your … ambition."

She glared at him, then shifted slightly, her gaze wandering to the sander in her hand. "If you must know—"

"I don't need to know."

She closed her mouth and pushed her hat back slightly, looking down at him through those long lashes. "Well, then. I'll get back to my work on the railing."

He nodded, but didn't move.

She scowled, one brow lifted. "So, you can go now."

"Maybe I'd like to watch awhile."

She tilted her head. "So you can learn a thing or two?"

Silence, followed by laughter, rolled out of Jake. "Fine. You win. May I ask why you're working on this side of the house?"

The sun beat down on both of them. She reached for her hat and pressed it down hard on her head. "I don't understand your question."

"Damage is on the other side."

"True, but you know the rules. I need a permit."

"Ah."

She flipped stray tendrils of hair over her shoulder. "Just so happens I'm waiting for the city to release the permit for the work that needs to be done over on that side. I've hired a friend of mine, a handyman, to help me get it done fast so my mother can move back in."

Jake rubbed his chin. "Permitting process can take a long time. Need a hand with it?"

"No, thank you. I've got it covered."

"Because I'm going over there tomorrow anyway. I could check on your permit for you."

"Look, Jake, I appreciate the offer. But I would prefer to see this project through from start to finish on my own."

"Understood." He backed away. "Enjoy your evening. And by the way, I'm not in the market right now."

Daisy scrunched her nose. "Excuse me?"

He raised both eyebrows. "For the house."

If she responded, Jake didn't hear it. He entered his family's beach house, a strange grin still stuck on his face. How he needed that. Between the prospect of staying in the old place for the next month, and the cloud of pending fines and a potential lawsuit hovering over him, Jake had not laughed in months. And smiles came at a premium.

He glanced out the window at the girl in the cowboy hat swinging a sander. Good thing she hated him as much as she did. Not that he was looking. As he'd said ... he wasn't in the market.

But if he were interested, he wasn't about to bring a beautiful woman into his troubles. That wouldn't do at all.

DAISY HAD HER RITUALS. She rolled her toothpaste tube from the bottom. Always put moisturizer with sunscreen on her face. And she never started her day without hot coffee spiked with oat milk, a custom she acquired while traveling in Sweden.

Today, though, would be a first. She should have known better than to put her faith in her mother's vintage four-cup coffee maker. The thing sputtered and groaned to a halt halfway through the coffee-making process and practically begged her to send it to the landfill. Well, if the thing could talk it would have. She huffed a sigh. Truth was, if she were to remove the relic from the house, her mother would undoubtedly ask about it. And Daisy would get the blame.

Resigned, she unplugged the machine and wandered

outside. A haze of morning greeted her, as did a whoosh of waves roaring onto the shore. She leaned onto the newly sanded deck rail and closed her eyes, letting the slightly salty breeze embrace her face.

Something about that sound from her childhood swept away her problems. At least for the moment. She'd forgotten about its power, about the way she would wake up as a kid and throw open her window to let that thunderous sound in. Unlike her friends who pulled the covers over their heads at the first sign of morning, Daisy liked to throw them off and see what the day had brought.

She still woke up early, even now, but Daisy couldn't remember the last time she did so with any panache. Maybe it was time to start.

After dashing inside for a handful of bills and her camera, Daisy walked east toward town. She had messed with that broken-down coffee pot so long that, surely, some-place in town would be open by now. She wandered past quiet homes, their windows burnished with awakening, and every now and again she'd catch signs of life—an elderly gentleman checking the porch for his newspaper, a child running past an open window, the start of a car engine in a driveway. Even that old church in the meadow seemed to be more awake now than the last time she'd seen it. She slowed in front of it and snapped a few photos.

Daisy turned the last corner and drifted along the main drag that led away from the beach. If she didn't find some-thing on this stretch of town, she could always walk up to the corner and turn onto Colibri Boulevard, which, despite its name, was no wider than a single lane on each side.

Fortunately, she didn't have to take another step. She

entered Brooke's Beachside Bakery and followed the aroma of freshly ground coffee beans. A young woman greeted her. Her name tag read Hattie.

"Good morning. What can I get you?"

Daisy's eyes took in the muffin tops and coffee cakes and other baked goods. But first, coffee. "Some of that amazing smell would be just perfect," she said.

Hattie laughed. "It is amazing, isn't it? Would you like a cappuccino? Or a latte? Our new espresso machine is state-of-the-art."

"Really! Well, anything would be better than my mother's sorry old coffee pot at home, so why not go for the best? I'd love a cappuccino, except ... you don't happen to have oat milk, do you?"

"Of course, we do."

Daisy blinked, momentarily frozen. They have oat milk. "That's the best news I've heard in days."

Hattie smiled. "Glad to hear that. Anything from the case this morning?"

Daisy considered all the yummy pastries behind the glass, but realized she couldn't eat them all. Well, she shouldn't. But one couldn't hurt ... "How about a custard-filled croissant?"

"Great choice."

Daisy paid for her items and glanced around. An over-sized chalkboard hung on the wall with words written with a flourish: *Gratitude is happiness doubled by wonder* - Chesterton.

"Why don't you find yourself a table and I'll bring your breakfast to you," Hattie said.

"Perfect."

She found a spot by a window. There was a sleepiness to the town, a reflection on the time of year, she thought. Fewer cars drove by than she would expect during other seasons. She hadn't been home much in the past few years, but some things never changed. Except, maybe, for the addition of this bakery to the town.

"Here you are." A different woman delivered her coffee and croissant. "I'm Brooke. Anything else I can get you this morning?"

Daisy smiled. "No, this is perfect. Is this your place?"

The young woman beamed. "It is. We've been open for a few months. First time in?"

"Yes. Although I grew up around here. The town is virtually the same from when I was a kid. Except for this place, I mean."

"I hear you. I'm not from here, but I used to visit my grandmother in the summers, too, so this area has always felt a little like home to me. Especially now."

"Well, your place fits right in here. It's homey. Welcoming."

"Thank you so much." Brooke turned to leave, then paused. "Since you grew up around here, I wonder if you know my friend, Lea Dorsey?"

"I do! Well, sorta. She was my grandmother's neighbor and sometimes brought over zucchini from her mom's garden." Daisy waved a hand. "I don't know if she would remember me, though. I'm younger and always felt a little, I don't know, invisible I guess."

Brooke smiled kindly. "You'd be surprised. She actually works for me part time, so maybe you can test her memory out one of these days."

The bell on the bakery door rang and both women turned, but the instant Daisy saw who stepped inside, she shrank behind Brooke. Too bad invisibility cloaks weren't real.

Brooke eyed the woman and quipped, "You're a fan of Lillian's too, I take it?"

"Avoiding her like the flu."

Brooke nodded, a knowing smile on her lips. "If only a simple mask and hand sanitizer could repel her."

Daisy suppressed a laugh. No need to draw the town's somewhat notorious realtor's attention. The woman had left her mother several messages. Daisy had deleted them all.

"Enjoy your breakfast, Daisy. Hope to see you back in again soon."

Daisy turned toward the window, hoping Lillian wouldn't notice her taking surreptitious bites of the most decadent croissant she'd ever tasted. Vive la France! The coffee went down smooth and creamy, and she had to control herself or she might have inhaled it in one sip. Not that moving quickly would have been a bad idea.

Unfortunately, she wasn't quick enough.

Lillian Madsen approached Daisy wearing spiked leopard-print heels like she was attending a conference in Vegas, rather than schlepping around the beach town so early in the morning. She gestured to the empty seat at Daisy's table. "May I sit, Daisy?"

She didn't wait for Daisy's answer, which, of course, would have been yes. She wasn't rude. But ... really? Interrupting a person's breakfast indulgence to meddle?

Brooke reappeared, silently poured a cup of coffee for Lillian, and slipped away.

Lillian zeroed in on Daisy. "What brings you into this establishment so early?"

Daisy hid her surprise at the woman's use of her name, although on second thought, it was probably Lillian's aim to know everybody in this one-seagull town.

"I've always been an early riser."

"That's nice." She sipped her black coffee. "How is your mother, dear?"

"She is improving every day. Thank you for asking."

Lillian tilted her head, a half-smile on her face that reminded Daisy more of pity than it did joy. "That's good to hear. It is so difficult when our parents begin losing their health."

Daisy took a sip of her cappuccino, unsure of how to answer that. Lillian had been around since she was a kid—and she'd thought of her as old then. And if she was not mistaken, didn't Lillian have an adult son and daughter? Hm. She wondered if they were concerned about their mother's ... health.

"Well," Daisy said, "I'm just so happy that she's doing better and will be home soon."

"Speaking of home, dear, what are your plans?"

Daisy took a slow sip of her coffee, then nonchalantly said, "Plans?"

"Why, yes. I hear your mother's home needs extensive work. Certainly not something for a young woman like yourself to handle."

"Why not?"

Lillian blinked. Clearly, she wasn't used to a "young woman" like herself answering back so quickly.

She recovered, that same patronizing look safely back on

her face. "You could, of course, handle anything that came your way, but why would you want to? Your mother had a stroke and I would think that for your own peace of mind—and for hers—you might want to consider Jade Gables as a suitable home for Wren."

"The old folks' home?" Daisy shook her head, a million thoughts crisscrossing their way through her mind. Like, how her mother could even be old enough to consider such a move. She couldn't fathom it.

Lillian attempted to laugh away Daisy's concerns. "Dear, Jade Gables is an assisted-living facility. Your mother would have her own room there. She'd have friends and caregivers. Really, you could not go wrong."

Daisy snapped a look at the interloper who had interrupted her breakfast and who was attempting to derail her plans—her mother's plans. "She wouldn't have the beach," Daisy said.

Lillian stared back at her. With barely a blink this time, she reached into her pocket and placed her business card on the table between them. She slid it over to her. "I can assure you that I have your mother's best interest at heart. I can sell the house for top dollar, enough to pay for everything she would need at Jade Gables, including a chauffeur to take her to the beach anytime she would like to go."

"No, thank you."

Lillian's forehead bunched like a Shar-Pei. "You can't be serious."

The bakery door opened and a familiar man strolled in. Daisy couldn't place him but was glad for the distraction, and she took the opportunity to stand, leaving Lillian's card on the table.

"Don't forget my card, dear," Lillian said, holding it out to her.

Daisy toyed with repeating the words, *no thank you*, when the man noticed them. He pivoted away from the bakery counter and approached. "Hello, Mother," he said, and kissed Lillian on the cheek.

"Good morning, Trent."

That's right. His name was Trent. He had been one of the older guys in town, one of the cute boys that flirted with all the girls on the beach. Well, the ones that could fill out bikinis. Unlike her.

Daisy dared to remember those days, when she was the munchkin among models. She had worn a one-piece through high school, trying to hide the fact that she was flat as a crepe on top. Short, flat, and shapeless. Good thing memes had not been a thing back then because she was pretty sure her photo would have shown up on the internet with that moniker plastered across her picture.

Trent looked at her, momentarily resting his chin on one bent finger. He snapped his fingers. "Daisy Mcafee!"

"That's me."

"Nice to see you again." He glanced at his mother and a silent message seemed to pass between them, one she could not precisely translate. On second thought, that wary look he gave his mother may have been a warning.

"You too, Trent," she said, trying not to sound pathetically enthusiastic over the fact that he remembered her. She picked up her coffee and the remnants of her breakfast. "Have a lovely day."

Daisy dashed out the door and didn't bother to look behind her. Once home, she showered, grabbed her car, and headed out to hunt for inexpensive decor. The unfortunate meetup with Lillian spurred her into action, and she hoped to find items she could use to brighten up the house for her mother's eventual return.

She also placed a call to her friend, Rafael, the handyman she'd lined up after they'd attended a wedding together recently—the infamous day that Jake had caught her up on that ladder. She bit her lip thinking about that, then shoved the memory away. She had told Rafael on the phone that work on her mother's house would start soon. As she pulled into a parking place, she hoped that what she told Rafael was correct—that the city would be issuing her permit ... fast.

JAKE STARED at the computer screen, four sets of eyes focused on him. His lawyerly sister Grace watched him intently whenever he spoke. If this was how it felt to be on the witness stand, he wanted no part of court proceedings anytime soon.

He and his sisters had started these weekly video calls when Grace moved to the beach house for her month-long stay. They usually pulled the calls together on Sunday nights, but Lacy, who worked in hotel sales, had been on a plane to New York during what would have been their usual meeting—the reason they were all staring at each other on a Monday night.

"How fast will you be able to turn the place around?" Maggie asked him.

Jake tapped his pencil on the legal pad in front of him,

the to-do list growing at a rapid rate. He'd spent the past couple of days scrutinizing the house in daylight and that alone added a page to the list in front of him. He would take care of a million small things—like ramping up the Wi-Fi while he was here. In the end, though, he had decided to pour most of his focus into the kitchen. "I'm putting in new cabinets and appliances this week and next."

"Too pricey," Maggie said.

Grace cut in. "Trust me, the kitchen needs an update." While spending her month at the beach house, she had been put in charge of the initial list-making, and Grace had made it clear that the place needed work. Not that he had been surprised.

Bella's wide-eyed pout dominated the screen. "I thought you didn't want to sell the house, Grace."

Grace gave their youngest sister a sympathetic smile. "It's not that I want to, necessarily, but it would probably be best for all of us if we do."

Though she said the words, Jake sensed some hesitation in them. Grace hadn't wanted to spend a month at the house when she did, mainly because she had just landed her dream job.

A whole lot of wrangling had happened during his sister's month in Colibri Beach, and if he had to guess, Jake believed she might actually like to keep the place in the family. But she knew the others either did not want to—him, for example—or that they felt they could not afford to.

Lacy had been silent throughout most of the conversation. The jet-setting hotelier had been sipping wine and nodding occasionally throughout the call, her dark hair pulled back severely. She was the only one who reclined on the couch during these calls while the others appeared unnaturally close to the screen.

Finally, Lacy said, "I agree with the new kitchen. Check. What's up next?"

Grace frowned, focusing on Lacy. "Are we keeping you from something?"

Lacy set down her glass and let one arm loll behind her head. She yawned. "Maybe I just don't want to stay in a rickety old house when it's my turn. Hear that, Jake? I need you to get that place in shape for me."

Maggie shook her head. "It's going to take a lot of money to fix up the place and I, for one, don't have it."

Lines traversed his oldest sister's forehead. He'd sensed for some time that life wasn't exactly a party for her. Not that he expected being a single mother would be. But he had noticed her fretting on these calls more often than not, and that had led him to suspect it wasn't from sheer bossiness, though she had displayed plenty of that growing up.

Jake shifted. "Don't worry about the cost—"

Grace cut in. "Don't forget about the budget."

"I haven't," Jake said. "I have some favors owed me. Plus, as stipulated in our parents' will, I'll be providing most of the labor myself." It wasn't exactly a lie. He did have plenty of people in his profession who believed they owed him something—their words, not his. His sisters didn't need to know where his financing came from.

Lacy leaned toward her computer camera. "Perfect, Jake. Now if you'll all excuse me—"

Someone pounded on Jake's door. He frowned.

Maggie squinted into the camera, as if that could help her see across the room. "Are you going to get that?"

He shook his head. "Probably someone selling ency-clopedias."

Bella sighed. "I bet they're vintage."

Maggie snorted. "Encyclopedias have gone the way of VCRs."

Grace laughed. "Maybe, but you should see some of the thick volumes of research books we have in our law office. They're worth hundreds each."

"You mean they cost hundreds," Maggie said.

Jake slid a look at Lacy. "What were you saying when we were interrupted?"

Someone pounded on the door again, this time louder and for a sustained time. Jake looked into the screen. "Hang on a second." He covered the room in three long strides and swung open the door.

"You did this!" Daisy hurled herself toward him, bumping into his chest, and when he didn't step back, she shoved a piece of paper at his face.

Jake's eyes ran across the document. He winced. The Mcafee house had been red-tagged. He shot her a look. "Daisy, I didn't have anything to do with this. Why would you think that?"

Half circles hung beneath her eyes. "Because you said you were going to the planning office today. Even if you didn't do it on purpose—"

"Which I wouldn't do."

She snapped those eyes at him. "Then you must have said something to somebody about our property."

He reached out to her, but she ducked beneath his outstretched arm. A tug in his middle wanted to comfort the girl he'd known years ago, though maybe "known" wasn't exactly the right term according to her. He slid a glance to where she retreated into the dining room, her arms hugging herself. In retrospect, no touching was best. They should stay a body's length apart. He would be here only a short time, then head back into the abyss of problems at home. He'd be no help to her.

And vice versa.

She whispered, "If you said something to them, I swear, Jake..."

Lacy's voice cut in. "Knock-knock. Yoo-hoo. What kind of trouble have you gotten yourself into now, big brother?"

Daisy jerked a look around the corner.

Jake gave her an awkward smile. "Video call with my sisters." He strode to the computer. "You all remember Daisy, don't you?"

Daisy stepped tentatively in front of the screen. "Hey, ladies," she said, her voice subdued.

"Oh my gosh, Daisy!" Bella said. "Haven't seen you in so long!"

"Sweet, Daisy," Maggie said. "Hello."

Grace smiled at her sympathetically. Jake knew that Grace and Daisy had spoken on the phone after Wren's stroke, but he didn't think they'd had much contact since then. "Good to see you, Daisy. How's your mother?"

"She's improving. I'll always be grateful to you and your husband." She wiped away a tear that streamed down her cheek, and, once again, Jake found himself fighting the urge to wrap an arm around her, to offer her some kind of comfort.

"And what is happening with your house?" Grace asked, pressing her gently.

Daisy held up the red-colored tag. "I've been notified that I need to vacate, which will make it hard for me to get the place ready for my mom to come home. They even had the electricity shut off!" She sniffled and righted her shoulders. "It's for something that makes no sense at all."

Jake held out his hand. "May I?"

Daisy turned to him, distrust in her eyes, and something painful twisted in his chest. She relented and handed him the document.

"You know, our boy Jake'll help you," Lacy said. "I believe he has some connections when it comes to building issues, right, brother?"

Jake slid a glance at Lacy. Something about the way she eyed him made him cringe, like there was a deeper meaning to her words.

"I have an idea," Grace said. She wore that thoughtful lawyer look, the one that brought his hackles to attention. Somehow he knew that whatever his little sister said was going to involve him.

"You can stay in our place while you deal with the city. You can have the whale room that we all stayed in once upon a time." Grace turned her chin toward Jake. "I'm sure that will be fine with Jake."

Those hackles now stood at attention.

"Oh, that's a perfect idea!" Bella said.

"Yeah, I'd have to agree with Grace on that," Lacy said. She speared Jake with a look and held up her wineglass in a mock *salud*.

"Thank you for the gesture, Grace," Daisy said. "But I— no, I couldn't do that to, uh, Jake. I'll figure something out."

"Don't be silly," Bella said in that little girl voice of hers.

"Nostra casa è la tua casa—our house is your house. That's what our mother used to say."

Maggie sat back, sighing. "She certainly did—she even taught Dad that phrase and it stuck. Really, Daisy, the timing is perfect and we'll do whatever we can to support you. Won't we, Jake?"

All eyes were on him.

He tilted his gaze to Daisy. "Of course, we will," he said softly. "This is a big place. Drafty, but big. You are welcome to stay as long as you need to."

Lacy cut in again. "And Jake'll help you with the city's big, bad planning department."

He nodded, still questioning Lacy's motive. "I will, if you'll let me."

Truthfully, he did not care to have a housemate—he had plenty of work to do both on the family home and on the LA project breathing down his collar. But he knew how it felt to be falsely accused of something, and if his assessment of Daisy's red tag was correct, someone had stretched the truth.

Plus, if he were honest with himself, there was a comparable-value element at play. If, for some reason, Daisy were to sell the Mcafee house as-is, the value of his family home could be greatly reduced. Not that he needed money. Far from it. But there was an intrinsic value in the place that he and his sisters had called home each summer and he hated to see it go for a pitiable number.

"So," Grace said, "will you take us up on our offer?"

"Yeah," Lacy said, "will you move in with Jake?"

Daisy pressed her lips together, her eyes wide, a vague wrinkle forming between them. An intriguing, vague wrinkle. She took a tentative look at Jake, as if wondering how on board with this he really was.

He held her gaze. "It's the best solution, Daisy."

She nodded and whispered, "Thank you," but the expression on her face told him she felt as conflicted as he did.

DAISY STUFFED HER CLOTHES, toiletries, and tools into the old suitcase that her father left her, and whispered "Here we go" under her breath. Using her phone's light to guide her, she made her way inside the Holloway home, then down the creaky wooden hall of the old beach house. She'd been there before, of course, but it had seemed larger to her then. And foreboding, too.

Daisy blushed in the darkness, thinking of the way she pined for Jake as a teenager. He was three years older and, obviously, barely noticed her, choosing instead to hang out with tall, skinny girls in tiny, string bikinis.

Whatever.

He'd been traipsing behind her ever since she walked through the front door. He hovered in the doorway of the girls' old room. "Sure there's nothing back at the house that you would like me to get for you?"

She gave him a brief glance over one shoulder. "No, thank you."

"Tomorrow I'll stop by the planning department and snoop around. I won't mention that we've talked—no need to draw unnecessary attention to your situation."

Daisy listened to him in silence. He was ashamed of her

and her mother's home. Check. She appreciated the effort, even if it did feel forced and the message he sent was off-putting.

He shifted and she barely looked at him. "Well, then, good night," he said.

After he had gone, she wilted onto the bed, her things at her feet. The room was exactly as she remembered it, except for appearing smaller. Double bed, off-white bedspread with a fat, spouting whale on it. Sea glass green walls, white bookshelf, and wicker TV stand. The windows, however, looked newer than the house itself.

Her stomach grumbled and she realized, quite suddenly, that she hadn't eaten. She sneaked a look toward the doorway. She did not want to interact with Jake any more than absolutely necessary, but though it was only a little after nine o'clock, he had said good night and she remembered hearing his footfalls going up the stairs. As she recalled it, there was a master bedroom up there.

She tiptoed to the doorway and peeked out. Nothing. Daisy slipped out of her sneakers and padded down the hall in her socks. The wind had begun its nightly howl, slamming itself against the old house. Daisy shuddered. The wind, so typical for this stretch of the beach, had one positive outcome: tomorrow the sky would be clear and blue. But that force had also helped spread the fire that made its way to her mother's home last month.

As she stood in the living room now, debating whether to dart across the divide between the two houses to search for food, a car pulled into the driveway. She stepped back, watchful. A person stepped out of the car and shut the door. She held her breath, wondering. Was Jake expecting someone? Was there another roommate? Someone she did not know about?

The man rounded the car and bounded up the steps. He wore a blue baseball cap and smelled like ... pepperoni. "Evening."

"Hi." She noted the large pizza box in his hands. "Um, I think you have the wrong—"

Jake's voice cut in from behind her. "I'll take that. What do I owe you?"

After he paid for the pizza, Jake pivoted, box in hand. "Hungry?"

Yes, yes, she was. But she shook her head no anyway. "Thanks, but I'm fine."

His eyes brushed over her face. "You look hungry." Her stomach growled and he laughed. "Thought so. Join me?"

She shrugged. "Sure."

"Have a seat." He plopped open the pizza on the island and picked up a bottle of wine. "Chianti?"

When she didn't answer right away, he pulled two wine-glasses from a shelf and began to pour. He set a glass in front of her. "I'm not a fan of drinking alone."

"Thanks." She took a sip, her thoughts inundated with memories and worries. Jake was being nice to her. That's all. She had to keep her mind clear of the past, of the feelings she'd had for him way back when. This moment was a vapor that would soon pass and she'd better hang onto that fact so she didn't somehow get sucked into any other daydream.

"Can't believe this pizza place is still around." Jake dug into a slice of the pie. He looked thoughtful for a moment. "On second thought, I can. LA pizza can't compete."

"I doubt that."

"I would not lie to you. I have had pizza at just about every joint in the greater Los Angeles area and nothing tastes as good as"—he looked at the box lid—"Matty's Pizza."

"That's a lot of pizza."

He swallowed a bite and grinned. "It is."

She could do this if she really tried, talk to Jake Holloway over a pizza as if it were the most natural thing in the world. She picked up her wineglass. "Are you one of those bachelors who eats out every night?"

He pointed his slice of pizza at her. "Affirmative."

She gave him a surprised laugh, the feel of it liberating. "I was only kidding, but okay. Must be expensive to eat out all the time, especially in LA."

He shrugged. "I'm hardly ever home. I work long nights in my office and spend the bulk of my time out in the field. Last thing I want to do when I get home is cook."

Daisy nodded, finishing up her first slice.

"Have another." Jake slid a piece onto her plate.

Her mind flashed on the short girl in the one-piece swimsuit who often felt chubby.

Jake's brows rose. "You okay?"

Daisy shook away the memory. She'd have to run the food off tomorrow, but isn't that why she had taken up the sport in the first place? To leave her past body image behind? She snapped a look at him. "Yes, I'm fine."

Jake poured himself more wine and added to her glass, watching her. "How about you? You spend a lot of time in the kitchen?"

She stared at him.

"What?" He laughed, though it sounded guarded. "Did

that sound like some kind of anti-feminist remark or something?"

Daisy pushed her plate away from her. "I didn't say that."

He had stopped eating and was watching her now, a confused look on his face. "What is it you're not saying?"

Daisy slid off the counter stool, her appetite gone. It took too much effort to stay thin and curvy just to throw it away on pizza and the fake affection of her childhood crush. She put a hand on the counter. "Thank you for dinner, Jake. I think I'll go on to my—to Grace's room now."

"So that's it?"

Daisy narrowed her eyes at him. Was he expecting something more from this arrangement? Her lungs constricted. When she was young she dreamed that Jake would pay attention to her, but she knew better now. She'd learned to protect herself and her heart from men like Jake, and she wasn't about to reverse herself now.

She began to walk toward the hall. "I appreciate the food and the safe place to land. Good night."

Jake watched her with a wariness in his gaze, his eyes scrutinizing.

Daisy tried to ignore the suspicious expression he wore, but it dug at her. She stopped. "Why that look?"

"What look?"

"Like I'm ... I'm stupid or something. Am I not allowed my feelings?"

He scoffed. "You can feel or think anything you'd like. I don't know what you think you saw, but I did not have that ... that look you were describing on my face."

She flashed him a placating smile. "Whatever you say."

His forehead furrowed. "Daisy, you're acting rather paranoid."

"Oh really? Rather paranoid?"

He dumped a half-eaten piece of pizza into the box and shut the lid, shaking his head the entire time. "I realize that you've had a bad day, but not everyone is out to get you."

She rolled her eyes. Hard. "Oh please. Don't pretend to understand how I feel, okay, Jacob?"

He scowled. "It's Jake."

Daisy snickered. She remembered a lot about Jake—more than he probably thought possible—and one thing that lodged in her mind was how his father would call him Jacob whenever he was annoyed with him. Which, from what she recalled, was quite often. She also remembered how much Jake seemed to really, really hate it.

Jake grabbed a towel from the counter, wadded it up, and tossed it into the sink. He snagged her with a look. "It's going to be a long month."

Daisy stared back at him. "I'll say."

Silence shot between them.

Jake groaned. "Speaking of long month, I'm tearing out the kitchen tomorrow. I know that's going to make things even tighter around here."

"I'll be up and out of here early tomorrow anyway, so no worries about me."

Jake came around to the front of the island and leaned back against it. He crossed his arms and exhaled. "I'm sorry about what you are going through, especially in regard to the house. For some reason, you and I are, uh, not connecting all that well. Are we?"

"No." She looked down. "Not very well at all." Daisy's

mind tumbled backward. Jake used to play catch on the beach with whatever was around—balls, sticks, discs, and even seaweed bladders. He and the other guys would hurl themselves through the air to catch a long pass, often landing hard enough to cause the packed sand beneath her to rumble.

When the sun finally sank into the ocean and the glow of it had passed, they'd all disburse to their family homes. No one ever seemed to notice that she was still out there, beneath the big wide sky. Eventually, she'd pick up her things and wander home, hoping that the following day Jake would finally notice her.

She looked back up only to find Jake considering her. Part of her wondered what was going on in that handsome head of his.

The other part of her felt, well, quite stuck here in this house with him. True, she was grateful for a comfortable place to stay, for the Holloway sisters' generosity. But she no longer cared whether Jake noticed her or not. Her childhood crush was just that, and she had no intention of indulging in that fantasy ever again.

"Good night, Jake," she finally said. Daisy had learned to guard her heart, unlike when she was young and her dopey-eyed crush had torn her up inside. As she made her way back to the girls' old bedroom, she reminded herself that she would never, ever allow Jake to mess with her head again.

3

Early the next morning, Daisy met her friend, Rafael, outside of her mother's home. Rafael smiled kindly at her, his sea-gray eyes beautifully startling against golden brown skin. They'd known each other since elementary school—even though he was older—and whenever she was in town, they'd grab a coffee or something. That's why it had been so easy to throw on a dress and accompany him to his cousin's wedding the other day. He towered over her, no surprise there, and appeared eager to get started on the projects.

"I received some bad news yesterday." She held up the red tag for him to see. "The inspector had told me there shouldn't be any problems, but this appeared and now all my plans are messed up."

He gave her a regretful look. "Ah, you will need to go to the planning department today."

"Unfortunately, yes. But I have the restoration company coming this morning to pick up a ton of items so they can get the smoke out of them. Will you help me bring some boxes down from upstairs so I can go through them out here in the light?"

Rafael slid a look at the house, no doubt wondering what an inspector might say if they were to be found moving around inside.

Daisy touched his arm. "It will go much faster if we work together."

He nodded. "Yes, of course. Lead the way."

For the next hour and a half, she and Rafael carried boxes of clothing, purses, rugs, draperies, and other items down the stairs to the back porch. Even though she opened the westerly windows each day, the inside of the house still smelled like an ashtray—as did her own clothes and skin. By ten a.m., she already felt the need for a second shower and she was beginning to wonder how she had been able to sleep in this house prior to moving in with Jake.

Rafael set two full boxes onto the porch. He raked a hand through his full black hair, allowing extra-long snippets to fall in front of his chiseled face. She'd noticed more than one woman sneaking peeks of him while they were dancing at the wedding.

Daisy handed him a bottle of water.

"Thanks." He guzzled the water, then capped the bottle again. "Serge has a carpet cleaning business now. I could call him to get some of that smokiness out of the house."

Serge was Rafael's brother, who she didn't know all that well. "Really? Oh, that would be so, so great. Do you think he could come at the end of the week after I've had a chance to figure things out with the city?"

Rafael nodded, his eyes darkening. "Of course. I will talk to him."

"Thanks so much. I guess we're all done here for now. I'll wait for the restoration truck and then see what I need to do about that stinkin' red tag."

He hopped off the porch and waved to her as Jake emerged from the house next door looking like he had a scowl permanently affixed to his face. He crossed the divide between the properties, looped his muscular arms over the deck railing, and hoisted himself to stand on the protruding deck boards. He was covered in dust.

"Hey," she said, barely looking at him.

"I see you've been busy."

"Same with you."

"True." He smacked the dust from his hands. "Been over to the planning department yet?"

"Nope."

"Hm. Want me to go with you?"

She eyed him. Why was he being nice to her? Daisy shook her head and sent a puff of breath into the air. "The more I think about it, the more it's got to be some kind of misunderstanding. The house is smoky and all, but it's solid. The fire only scorched the exterior wall. It didn't penetrate the house at all. Electrical is fine, plumbing is intact." She shrugged. "I'm not too worried about it."

"I haven't wanted to pry—"

She shot him a look. "Then don't."

Jake pulled himself up and over the railing, landing with a thud, boots first on the deck. "Been thinking about your predicament and I think you should let your homeowner's insurance handle the dealings with the city."

She kept her eyes on the boxes on her deck. "Is that so?"

"They have the staff in place that knows the right things to say and when to say them. It's commonplace."

Daisy licked her lips. She moved two of her mother's leather purses from one box to the other and fought off a sneeze before saying, "It's under control, Jake."

He peered at her. "What insurance company are you working with on this?"

She wasn't a particularly angry person, but Jake's constant questions had managed to rake her ire. He didn't need to know the issues she had with insurance—or lack thereof. Daisy lifted her chin and glared at him. She would have liked nothing better than to have help in this situation, a sibling, a friend ... someone. But not Jake. The minute she bared her soul to him, she feared he would shrug it off like simple small talk.

"Doesn't matter anyway," she said. "I think I know who might be behind the problem with the city. A Realtor has been calling my mother and she even tried to give me her card the other day. If she's behind this, I'm going to find out."

He frowned. "Lillian Madsen?"

She twisted a haughty gaze at him. "Friend of yours?"

"Hardly." He paused, then shrugged. "She's a pain in the butt, but I seriously doubt she has that kind of pull with Colibri. Not a good idea to give her that kind of power."

"That's where you're wrong. I'm not the one giving her power, but if I were not to recognize her sneaky ways, she would be able to get away with all kinds of stuff. And I'm not going to let that happen."

Jake stared at her in that unnerving way of his, like she was cute but dumb.

She shoved one of the boxes with her toe, inching it toward the steps. "Knock that off. I'm not paranoid, in case you were thinking of bringing up that accusation again."

"I'm sorry I said that last night. Wasn't cool. But"—he quirked his head, his smile grim—"not everyone is out to get you."

She shook her head. "Typical."

"What do you mean?"

"Jake Holloway!"

He gave her a surprised laugh. "What?"

Daisy faced him now, her hand cupping her waist. "Okay, fine. We're going to go there."

"Um ..."

"Don't you remember that time you told me my sand-castle was dumb? When I was a kid?"

Slowly, his smile dimmed. "Daisy, what are you talking about? I don't remember that at all."

For some reason, his not remembering little things like that stung as much as when he'd hurt her feelings way back then. "My parents had been arguing so I slipped out of the house with a whole box of rakes and buckets. I spent all morning building the biggest, rambling compound on the beach out of sand."

"Wow."

"You just sniffed at it. Said, 'That's no castle. Where's the turret? And the ramparts?'" She shook her head, remembering. "I proudly told you that it was a ranch-style house with a barn. I even showed you all the little animals I made to graze around it."

He took a step closer to her, the familiar scent of him

both powerful and heady. Like musk and citrus. His voice was low. "What did I say?"

She stepped back and looked up at him. "You said, 'A sand ranch house? That's dumb.'"

He winced. "Really?"

She nodded, feeling kind of silly all of a sudden. "Yes. You did."

"Well," he said, his voice still low, still too lethal. "I don't remember that."

Daisy didn't answer him. She was too old to hold grudges from childhood. She knew this. But for some reason, seeing him again while in the midst of her tattered life brought up old hurts. And though she knew she should be far beyond this at her stage in life, Daisy found herself sinking under old disappointments.

He touched her shoulder, sending a shiver through her body. Even her toes curled. "Like I said, I don't remember that. But ... it sounds like something I would have said." He sighed. "I'm sorry, Daisy."

Daisy went silent. She'd expected resistance, maybe even some blustery denial, but never an apology. The simple words massaged their way through her, offering relief from the frenetic thoughts that had held her captive lately.

Maybe ... maybe it was time to end this one-sided war. He probably didn't even remember the rest of their story, as she often thought of it. She sighed. "Jake, we were kids." She licked her lips and forced herself to look up at him, the sun beginning to blur her vision. "I'm ready to move on and forget about it."

"It was still mean of me."

She laughed for the first time all morning. "Sure was. You jerk."

JAKE ROLLED over in the sheets, his legs entangled, the blare of his alarm shocking him into wakefulness. He punched his phone's alarm and stuffed a pillow under his neck. Daisy's face flashed into view, followed by the mug of that pretty-boy handyman she'd hired. He groaned.

What did it matter anyway?

Jake rubbed his eyes. His phone had been buzzing all night, but his mind had been elsewhere. Well, that had to stop. Immediately. The fortune he had built could very well disappear if he allowed himself to be derailed by ... a woman. Already this creaky old house had taken up far too much of his time, pulling him away from the pressing reality of litigious people.

With a groan, Jake hurled himself out of bed. He padded downstairs and into the kitchen—or what was left of it. Yesterday when he pulled out just about everything attached to the walls, he'd had the presence of mind to leave the coffee pot plugged in and sitting on top of a remnant of a cabinet.

He started up the pot and turned to his computer, still open on the kitchen island. Thirty-eight unopened emails— more than half, it seemed, regarding the legal issue that threatened to undo all that he had built. He blew out a long, hard breath. The need for coffee had dulled.

His phone buzzed. His assistant, Maisie, was on the line.

"Good morning, Jake!" she said.

"What's up?"

"What? No pleasantries?"

Silence.

She laughed lightly. "Fine! I get it—you're in vacation mode, but this is important, boss."

"Lay it on me."

He heard the sharp suck of air. "Really great news. I think." She squealed a little.

Jake felt the bunching of his forehead. "Are you going to share it with me or just hyperventilate?"

Another squeal, followed by sucking of air. "Okay. El Amor hotel chain wants to talk to you. Wait. Oh oh oh! It's more than that—I have it on good authority that they love your ideas for their property. Get it? Love ... amor? Anyway, my friend Emi's sister's roommate works as their executive assistant's assistant, and she said the owner was raving about your design, Jake. Is this the best news you've heard all day or what?"

He let her words sink in. They were a lifeline of sorts, pulling him from the mire of quicksand he'd found himself in lately. He combed a hand through his bedhead mop. If this were true, he would have something to think about other than the false accusations and governmental jostling he'd lately been buried under.

Not to mention the money that this project would guarantee. Not that he was hurting in that department. At least, not at the moment.

Minutes later, with a second mug of hot coffee in his hand, he stood at the picture window overlooking the sea. The ocean was swathed in pink from the eastern sky. Had he ever noticed this as a kid? His memories had more to do with joining his buddies out on the sand for a pick-up game of ... whatever.

Jake frowned. Daisy had a distinct memory of him. Eventually, he remembered the incident she recounted. Sort of. And another one niggled at him, too, though it wasn't as clear. For the past couple of days, life had lurched in a very different direction from when he'd arrived. He now found himself in the precarious place of sharing a home with a woman, a gorgeous woman, who appeared to, well, hate him.

On the one hand, he wasn't here for romance. Had too much on his mind to give a woman his full attention anyway. On the other, ever since he spotted her on that ladder—and then later on the beach—Jake had found himself captivated by the petite woman who, at every turn, seemed to want to beat him up.

He grinned. He could offer her an olive branch in the form of a piping hot cup of coffee ...

A masculine voice carried into the house from somewhere outside. Jake pulled himself away from the westward window toward the sounds of work and voices. He saw them through the window. Daisy was stepping into her mother's house through the deck, her so-called handyman following her inside.

Jake licked his top row of teeth, wondering. As far as he knew, she had not yet dealt with the city and their requirements for removing the red tag status of her home. If she were to be found trampling around inside, the powers that be wouldn't be so happy about it. Just might fine her.

He drained his coffee cup, and on his way out of the house, left it on a corner table. He slipped his feet into a pair of suede and canvas boat shoes and stepped outside.

Someone had to warn Daisy about the predicament she was putting herself—and Rafael—in. His shoulder tensed as he approached them. Who was he kidding? That guy could get arrested for all he cared.

"So anyway," Daisy was saying, "if Serge could be here early Friday morning, then I could leave the house open all—"

Jake stood in the doorway of Daisy's home, his arms folded at his chest. "Hello, roomie."

Daisy's expression darkened. "Did you want something?"

He flicked a glance at the guy by her side. Was standing pretty close for a handyman. "I'm headed over to the planning office." It was a lie, but she didn't have to know that. "Figured I'd offer to check in on your permit situation."

She shook her head. "Not necessary."

Jake opened his mouth to respond when Rafael cut in, completely ignoring him. He touched Daisy's shoulder, his hand lingering. "I'll give my brother your message. I have to stop by a job in town, but I will return." Rafael cast a warning glance at Jake before hopping off the porch.

After Rafael drove away, Daisy pivoted. Even with her face tipped upward, her chin barely reached the top of his chest. "You feeling really good about yourself right now?"

"What did I do?"

"Oh, come off it, Jake. I saw you giving Rafael the evil eye. What's that all about?"

He chuckled. "The evil eye? Like a cartoon character?"

She fumed.

He looked down at her through squinting eyes and wagged his pointer finger at her. "Wait. There. Okay, I got it."

"Got what?"

"You just gave me the evil eye." He cracked up. "Now I know what you were referring to."

She grabbed his finger and gave it a hard twist.

"Ouch!" Jake pulled his hand away, shaking it in the air. "You're brutal."

She stared at him, her chest rising and falling. A millimeter of a smile showed up briefly. "I've got work to do."

Her words sobered him. She was right. Her mother's house appeared to have escaped fairly unscathed by the fire, but he could tell by the condition of the place that it likely had far needier matters hiding beneath its not-so-sunny facade. The plumbing and wiring were probably at least as old as Wren, unless she and her husband built the place, which he doubted.

Daisy had been watching him in silence and Jake had to force himself not to reach over and graze her cheek with a brush of his fingers. He was used to women clinging to him, of randomly showing up, dressed to kill. Daisy, though, was different. To her, he was still the dumb kid from next door who ignored her for years.

Jake planted his feet firmly instead. "Sorry to have interrupted your ... work."

"That supposed to be an apology?"

It was supposed to be ... Apparently, though, he couldn't even get an apology right. He took a step back, his mouth grim. "Sorry." Then Jake turned, hopped over the rail onto the sand below, and headed back into his own mess of a house.

Daisy yawned. Though it was barely after noon, she had been up since sunrise planning her strategy and implementing it the best she could. After meeting with Rafael this morning, followed by that annoying exchange with Jake, she headed to the planning department to discuss the ridiculous red tag left on her door.

The woman at the counter peered down at her like a school principal at an elementary school child. *No way was this planning department counter regulation height.* Daisy stretched herself up on her tiptoes, noticing the tug on her calf muscles. Surely there was some kind of accessibility regulation against this treatment ...

The clerk, whose name tag read Mel, had the longest nails Daisy had ever seen. She shuffled through a stack of papers with her fingers tilted backward, those claws slicing the air. She stopped on a document and slid it out of the stack with the pads of her fingers. "Found it."

Daisy's breath hitched.

The woman pursed her lips, deep gouges forming around her mouth. She tapped the file with those curved nails as if it would help her better understand the document in front of her.

"Says here that the exterior siding isn't regulation."

Daisy frowned. "Okay."

The woman snapped a look at her. "You can't live in it until it's fixed."

"I see." She didn't really, but a warning in her gut kept her from crossing the line with this woman. "What is the process for having the red tag removed?"

"I just said it. You need to fix it."

Daisy nodded. "Yes, of course. So I guess my question is,

once the siding has been replaced, do I come here and ask for an inspector to come by and approve the work?"

The woman sighed, her neck sinking into her shoulders. "First, your contractor will need to apply for the permit by submitting the plans. Once it has been approved, and the work has been done, he can let our office know."

She went silent.

Daisy swallowed. "And so it's at that point that someone will come out to inspect the work, right?"

"Right." The woman tossed the file into a drawer and looked over Daisy's shoulder at the next person in line.

Daisy stayed put. "Before I go, can you tell me who it was that came out and inspected the house in the first place?"

The woman reached for the file, pursing her lips as she looked it over. "Doesn't say, but it looks like they're getting somebody out there today. You can ask him when he gets there. Next!"

An hour later, Daisy stood high up on her mother's ladder. From what she'd gathered, there was nothing at all wrong with the eaves of the home. Curls of dried paint dripped from them, which further proved to her that those boards had been on the home a long, long time. Probably original.

The sound of tires crunching on the driveway jolted her from her thoughts. From her vantage point, she couldn't see who had arrived, but her mind raced with possibilities. Maybe just a lost tourist, using her driveway to turn around. Or maybe it was the inspector from the planning department the scary woman had mentioned. Either way, she couldn't help but feel a wave of tension wash over her.

A man's voice interrupted her concentration. "Well, hullo there."

She turned, bumping the bill of her hat on a fascia board. "Can I help you?"

The man at the foot of the ladder peered up at her through round spectacles. With his starched white-collared shirt, pocket protector, and short-cropped hair that stuck up like fence posts, he reminded her of an animated cartoon character.

"I'm here to take a look at the work that's being done on your wall here."

Daisy frowned. "Who are you?"

"Jon Carnes. With city planning."

"About that ... I just came from there and was told that a permit had to be applied for first."

"That's true information."

Daisy leaned her hands on the top rung. "My, uh, contractor is working on it, well, he will be soon." She didn't want to outright lie.

He chuckled. "You know, you're much too young and pretty to be up there on that ladder. Why don't you hop down here and we'll go over the process, hm?"

Daisy was about to tell him where he could stick his process when she noticed Jake coming around the side of the house. If this inspector was a friend of his, she very well might not be able to hold her tongue much longer.

Carnes spun on his rubber heels. "Well, if it ain't Jake Holloway." He chuckled louder this time. "I suppose you've come over here to save the damsel. You'd better get her down from there before she hurts herself."

"Hello, Jon." Jake lifted his chin in Daisy's direction

before swinging it back in the inspector's direction. He was holding a small plastic-wrapped plate. "I was just stopping by to see if my neighbor here would like this sandwich I made. She's been working awfully hard out here. Was the least I could do."

Carnes's brows lifted so high Daisy thought his hair might slide off his head. He opened his mouth but slapped it shut again without adding whatever wisecrack he'd been thinking about. Daisy glanced at Jake. After their verbal sparring of the morning, she didn't particularly want to accept anything from him. But then again, it appeared that he had just shut down Mr. Inspector's derogatory mouth. Why not be grateful?

"Thank you, Jake. I am pretty hungry—how'd you know?"

He grinned up at her. "A hunch."

Carnes cleared his throat. "I've got another appointment to get to," he said, his marble eyes stern. "See that your contractor gets that permit application in soon." He shoved his notepad back into the pocket in his shirt, nodded at Jake, then trudged off.

When he'd gone, Jake held the ladder as Daisy climbed down. She jumped onto the deck from two rungs up.

"You have a thing with ladders, don't you?" Jake quipped.

"Maybe I was up there planning on where to put the turret."

He laughed and handed her the sandwich. "Good one. Hope you like turkey."

She tilted her head, eyeing him. It would be so easy to turn that statement around ...

He laughed again and pointed at her. "Don't say it."

This time, she couldn't help but laugh back. She plunked herself onto a little patch of sand and dug into the sandwich, thankful for sustenance. With each bite, she felt tension ebbing away.

Jake stood nearby, looking out to sea, seemingly at ease. She tilted up her face until the sun warmed her cheeks. Then she shaded her eyes. "You really didn't mean to bring this out to me, did you?"

Slowly, he brought his gaze to her. "Maybe." In a moment of perfect timing, his stomach growled.

She swallowed another bite, nursing a smile. "Really is good."

"You're enjoying this."

"I am."

He swiveled around, leaning a hip against the wall of the house. "Fine. I will admit that I made that sandwich for myself."

"Really."

He pushed off the house. "When I saw that guy drive up, I knew there'd be trouble. He's been around since I was a kid." Jake paused, then lowered his voice, which nearly sounded like a growl. "Never could stand that guy's arrogance."

Daisy sobered. She'd come here thinking she would fix things up and be on her way. But the wheels of Colibri had memories, apparently. That and governmental red tape, just like the big city. Dread trickled through her. "Thank you," she said, simply. At this moment, Jake wasn't the jerk teenager who made her feel small and invisible, but the neighbor who was being, well, neighborly. She appreciated that.

"I have a confession to make."

"I can't wait."

"There's this memory I have, though it's pretty watery." Jake darted his gaze out to the sea, his eyes shifting, as if uncomfortable. He swung it back to her. "Daisy, did you ask me out once?"

Her appetite disappeared. Daisy dropped the rest of the sandwich onto a napkin, her cheeks suddenly blazing. She had imagined this moment for years, only she would be gorgeous and rich and really, really nice. He'd be fat. Poor. Maybe even have a bald spot. Boy, would he be sorry when he realized he could have had ... her!

Instead, he was still hot. She was still short. And she was suddenly feeling downright ornery.

He continued. "I turned you down, didn't I?"

Sometimes facing a terrible memory was a way of weakening its power. She exhaled. "Yeah, Jake, you did. It was that year that your family stayed longer at the beach house, when your dad had found work around here." She paused. "I asked you to take me to my freshman dance."

He frowned, the whole of it marring his beautiful face. "What did I say?"

"You said, 'No thanks.'"

He winced. "Ouch. I was an—"

"Yes. You were."

Jake groaned then sighed. He lowered himself onto the deck next to her and turned, looking fully into her eyes. "I'm the one who missed out. I'm sorry I did that to you, Daisy."

"It was a long time ago."

"Doesn't make me any less of a jerk."

She slid a glance at him. "Apologizing about it does, though."

They sat next to each other for a few minutes, staring at the sea, both caught up in their own heads. After some time had passed, Jake said, "May I ask you a question?"

His voice yanked her out of her musings.

His eyes steadied on hers. "Why isn't your mother's insurance company handling all of this for you?"

Daisy broke eye contact with him. She picked up the sandwich again and took the last bite of it, the events of the past few weeks settling on her shoulders. She sighed. "Not using any. My mother made the decision a while ago to drop the coverage to the bare minimum. She also raised the deductible to an outrageous sum. She's petrified that they'll raise the rates even higher if I were to call them." She shrugged and swung her gaze up to meet his. "Thought I could come out here and just take care of it myself, but I guess that's not working out as expected."

A range of emotions passed across his face, but Daisy didn't care if she'd shocked him. She came to do a job, and though she had hit some bumps along the way, she had no thought of giving up now.

He squatted down on his haunches, the strength in his quads apparent. She nearly lost her ability to breathe.

"Tell you what." He was face-to-face with her now. "Let me apply for the permit for you. I'll draw up some plans and stop over there in the morning. Won't leave until they hand it to me."

She licked her lips, aware of him watching her. Man, how she needed some water. "Why would you do that, Jake?"

He quirked a smile at her. "Maybe 'cause I'm sick of looking at this broken-down place."

Daisy narrowed her eyes before finally giving up. She laughed. "Fine. You win. I'll take you up on that!" Then she gave him a playful shove on his shoulder and watched him tumble backward onto the sand.

4

The next morning, Jake waited in line at the city planning office, his thoughts consumed by Daisy. After learning about her predicament with insurance brought on by her mother's decisions, he could barely contain his criticism. Of all the foolish decisions! But, he knew better than to share his thoughts about that. In reality, he found it incredible that she was trying to renovate her property and handle the city regulations on her own. Well, with the help of that pretty boy handyman she'd hired.

Jake wanted to roll his eyes, but considering he was inside a government office waiting his turn, he controlled himself. That and the fact that he was a grown man. His mind reflected back on Daisy eating that sandwich he'd brought her, her expression a mix between crestfallen and pride. When she'd told him her story, he felt ill-equipped to walk that tightrope of emotion and unable to take that first step. But then she had gifted him with a wide-eyed gaze,

probably the first time he had seen her let down her guard
since they had become ... reacquainted.

And he couldn't help her fast enough.

The person in front of him moved away from the counter
and he stepped up.

"Jake Holloway!" the clerk said. "How're you doing,
handsome?"

He grinned. "Never been better, Mel. Nice to see you
again."

The woman dropped her pen on the counter with a
clatter and walked around it. Jake had been to the planning
office many times with his father, and in this case, it was
good to see that some things never changed.

"Oh you are a sight for sore eyes!" Mel hugged him hard
against her full chest, squeezing the air right out of his lungs.
As a kid, he was no match for Mel's powerful embrace, his
face often landing awkwardly in her cleavage. Embarrassed
him to no end back then, although he vaguely remembered
bragging about it later as a teenager.

When she released him, he chuckled. "You look exactly
the same, Mel. And your hugs haven't changed much either."

She was on her way back to her desk when she stopped
short. "Much? You want me to hug you again?"

Silence fell between them and she broke out in that belly
laugh of hers. He watched her take her place behind the
counter, slip on her reading glasses, still sighing from
laughter.

"Now," she said, "what can I help you with? You adding
on to your parents' old place, God rest their souls?" She
made the sign of the cross on herself.

"I'm not here for myself, Mel, but for my neighbor."

She scrutinized him. "Your neighbor?"

"Yes. Wren Mcafee owns the house next door and the place experienced a fire not long ago. Are you aware of it?"

"My, yes. I read about that in the paper. If you're here for her, then she must've survived that stroke. My goodness! That was sad to hear about."

He pushed aside his personal feelings about Wren. "Yes, yes, she did. Her daughter Daisy is in town, trying to get the place fixed up, but she needs a permit for some exterior siding. Can you help us out?" He slid an application in front of her.

Mel sighed and placed one arm on top of the other on the counter. "Now what're you doing working on such an itty-bitty project? Didn't I read somewhere that you're in the big time now? That you've got your own company down in the City of Angels, and you're building skyscrapers and all kinds of state-of-the-art buildings?"

He smiled at her, glad that's all she'd read. "Never too busy to help a friend."

She pursed her lips and reviewed the application. "Hmm." Mel looked up. "So you're gonna supervise this?"

"Yes, ma'am."

She clucked. "Don't yes, ma'am me. That girl was in here the other day lookin' all flustered about this." Mel leaned closer, her eyes big and imploring. "She was pretty cute, too. What's her name again?"

"Daisy."

Mel laughed again, heartily. She shook her head. "If this isn't the sweetest thing."

He leaned casually against the counter, grinning. "I appreciate your help, Mel."

She filled out the permit and smacked it with a big rubber stamp. "Yeah, I just bet you do."

Twenty minutes later Jake pulled into the drive of his family's beach house. He didn't bother to go inside, but instead crossed the divide, permit in hand. On the ride over, he had decided to offer more help to her. No way would he allow Daisy to put that siding up there all by herself, especially up at the top. The danger of it all sent a shudder through him. His vow to help meant delaying his own project some, but if they worked together, he felt sure they could have it done quickly.

He stopped short.

Rafael was around the back, stacking fiber-cement siding beneath the deck. He was humming something Jake didn't recognize and had, apparently, forgotten to wear a shirt again.

Daisy skipped out of the back door with a pitcher and a cup. She allowed the screen door to slam behind her. "Hey, Jake."

Rafael swung around at the sound of Daisy's voice. He pulled off one of his gloves and wiped it across his brow in slow motion. Then he flashed Daisy a smile and took the cup from her, waiting as she filled it with water.

Jake's stomach roiled.

Daisy gasped. She jogged over to him, the pitcher still in her hand. "Don't tell me you got my permit!"

He smiled and put it behind his back. "Okay."

She reached for it. "Jake Holloway!"

He held it up in front of her. "Got it."

She squealed. "Oh my gosh! You're a miracle worker." She paused. "Did you have to pay them off or something?"

"Something like that."

Her eyes grew big. "Really?"

"No. The paperwork was in order, so there was no good reason for them to turn down the permit." He did not add that he'd had to suffer through one of Mel's bear hugs as part of the bargain. "Surprised you bought the siding already. Need help installing it?"

Daisy waved a hand casually in front of him. "I had faith in you. And no worries. Rafael and I are going to work on putting it all up there together. Phew, though. This permit came in the nick of time!" She reached for it. "May I?"

He handed the permit to her and cast a look over at her handyman, who stood there holding an empty cup and wearing a stupid grin on his face.

Jake was no longer needed.

He backed away. This was for the best. Jake owed his lawyer a phone call, he had email to answer, and if he ever wanted to cook a meal in the family beach house again, he knew he had better get moving. He stuck a hand in his pocket and turned to Daisy. "If you're sure, then—"

"We're good," she said, waving him off. As he turned away, he noticed that she had already joined Rafael underneath the deck.

HOURS LATER, Jake held his phone up in the empty kitchen, scanning the space. "What do you think, Mags?"

"I think anything looks better than those old cabinets and counters. Even nothing."

He grinned. Two of his other sisters would likely agree,

though the third, Bella, would no doubt have a hard time seeing their old family kitchen this way. He had a soft spot for his youngest sister, even though she was an unrealistic dreamer at times.

He turned the phone around so he could see Maggie. "You're mighty chipper."

She quirked her head. "Am I?"

"With all due respect, my sister, you usually have some sort of, hm, how do I say this?"

"Criticism to share?"

"That's it. You usually have something constructive to add after your compliments. Which, by the way, are usually few and far between."

"I'm hurt."

"You're not."

She threw back her head, laughing in that robust way of hers. As he listened to the sound of it, the front door opened. Daisy wandered in, moving tentatively across the space. Their gazes collided as she passed by, the moment sending an electrical current through him.

She didn't stop. Instead, Daisy headed toward the hallway, a slight limp in her gait, her eyelids drooping. Tension spread across his back and up his neck. Maybe he should have chased away that pretty boy and helped Daisy himself. She looked as if she could use a long nap and he hoped, for her sake, that she wouldn't emerge from her room anytime soon.

"So anyway," Maggie said, drawing him back into the conversation, "how are you really doing over there? I'm worried that your money's going to run out, Jake. I ... I wish I could help."

It was the closest she had ever come to admitting how difficult her finances had become. If Jake didn't have such a good friend at her bank, he would never have found out just how close she was to poverty.

"Maggie, I have it covered. Really."

"But you're doing the work and paying for it."

"I'm actually enjoying it." He swept a glance across the bare room, imagining the possibilities. "I haven't done this kind of work in years. Thought I'd never miss it, frankly."

"So it's ... therapeutic?"

He smiled. "Kind of, yeah."

She let out a long sigh. "If Dad could hear you now."

Jake's shoulders stiffened at the mention of their father. How many times had he stood in this very room, his feet shoulder-width apart, arms crossed in front of him, listening to his father's berating? Far too many.

After he and Maggie said their goodbyes, he unclenched his teeth and shook away his negative memories. His father was a good man, had taught him much, though he had been stubborn. Something they finally had in common.

Jake had always wanted to design buildings and homes and complexes. He wanted to put his wild ideas to paper and watch those creations take shape by someone else's hand. Not because he was lazy, as his dad sometimes alluded to. Nor because he was inept, a thought that Jake secretly wore at times. It was because his mind moved fast, like a shot that rang out in the East followed by another in the West. By the time all the permits and teams were in place to build what he had envisioned, he wanted to have moved on to his next project, his next fantastical idea.

The quick pace had served him well, though no one in

his family knew exactly how well. How would they feel if they knew he could buy their parents' home and hand it back to all of them without missing a dime? That he could buy it hundreds of times over? Not that doing so was an option—his parents had seen to that by writing their will the way they had.

A sobering gratefulness filled him. He glanced around the room. Some might only see the bareness of it all and declare it empty. Plain. Insufferably unlivable. His shoulders began to fill with oxygen, relaxing, because as Jake took it all in, he saw the possibilities.

His sister's words rang out in his head. *So it's ... therapeutic?*

Jake pressed his lips together, thinking. His sister needed more help. He knew it by her bank account balance, the way it hovered dangerously over the color red, but also by the wistfulness in her voice. When was the last time Maggie had a day all to herself? Didn't women like pampering?

He scowled, his mind detouring toward some of the women who had attempted to date him. The makeup ... the clothes ... the suffocating perfume! Wasn't exactly what he meant or wanted for his sister. Now that he thought about it, many of those women seemed to appear in the middle of his workday, for no apparent reason, dressed to someone's idea of perfection.

Jake leaned his bum against the single cabinet he'd left behind to hold coffee. A memory caused a curl of a smile to find him. The first time he'd seen Daisy—well, the first time in many years—she'd been wearing a knockout of a dress and tottering on heels. Somehow, that didn't bother him. With a start, he realized he had no idea where she had been going that day, dressed like that. A date? He cringed at that thought.

Of course, that was before he knew she was the munchkin from his childhood, the word bringing a slight chuckle out of him. The more he knew Daisy, the more annoyed he became with himself. Why had he been such a beast as a child? A teen? He hadn't had too many girlfriends —hadn't had the time. He'd been a serious one, with many goals. Women weren't one of them, although, admittedly, they had always been a pastime.

Jake sighed. If he weren't so overwhelmed and stressed with the pending fines, maybe he could explore something more ... permanent. He tossed away his musings, reminded once again of his sister's predicament. A quick look at his phone told him his friend at the bank would be going home soon. Jake leaned forward and peeked toward the empty hallway. He had heard nothing from Daisy since she wandered past him ten minutes earlier.

Quietly, he slipped out of the house and onto the front porch and dialed his friend.

Daisy awoke to the sounds of gulls cawing and drool puddling on her pillowcase. Her nap had been that good. She opened one eye, then the next. Feet on the floor again, she padded across the room, the house noticeably quiet. She had hit a wall earlier this afternoon, metaphorically speaking, and it was all she could do to drag herself back to the Holloway house and get some sleep.

Now up, she heard the muffled but unmistakable tone of

Jake's voice coming from somewhere outside of the living room. Funny how his voice hadn't changed much over the years. Nor had her reaction to it. Daisy's heart still stirred when she heard him speaking, as it had back when he used to so carelessly call her munchkin.

Idly, she tucked a wisp of hair behind her ear. She had more to accomplish tonight at her mother's home, but going outside would mean encountering Jake when she still felt a little groggy and emotionally raw.

She took a step toward the front door, which stood ajar.

"We'll do this as before, right?" she heard Jake saying. "Must be strictly anonymous."

Daisy froze. Did she dare step out on the porch now while he was so obviously in the middle of a business call? She sighed. She already felt like a reluctant intruder in his life, his home. How awkward was this? She leaned toward the door anyway, listening.

Jake sighed. "That's a legitimate question, Stu. One of these days I'll tell Maggie that I'm the one who's been providing her some help, but not now. She's stubborn and might not take me up on my offer, quite frankly."

Daisy frowned. Who was Stu? How was Jake helping Maggie? More than that, how could his sister not know if she was being helped? Daisy squeezed her eyes shut, pressing away lingering fatigue.

Jake continued. "Thank you, Stu. I appreciate your help again with this transaction." He paused, and then chuckled. "Well, that's the reason you've been my banker for all these years."

After Jake said goodbye, Daisy pushed open the screen door and stepped onto the porch.

He swiveled toward her, phone in hand, his expression moving from surprise to benign in a blink. "Hey."

She swallowed back a sigh, considering him. The late afternoon sun highlighted the shadow of whiskers on his handsome face. Much as she wished this not to be the case, he was still cute. And magnetizing ... shoot, he was downright sexy. She forced a look across the sand toward her mother's house. Allowing him to see the girlhood crush that showed up on her face periodically, like a bothersome blush, didn't seem like such a great idea.

Finally, Daisy corralled her wayward attention and drew her gaze back to Jake. At the same moment, he stood and shoved the phone into his back pocket, his eyes on hers.

Steady, steady. She would not be going there. Her mind whirred. What had she been thinking about when she first walked out onto this porch? Oh right. The phone call. She made herself breathe. Refocus. Was he really giving money to Maggie without her knowing it? "Sorry to interrupt," she finally said, her voice a squeak.

"No problem. I just finished up a call." He slid a hand into his front pocket, still watching her. "Did you have a good rest?"

"Yes, yes, I did." She paused, thinking. "Learned a while ago that the secret to productivity is a twenty-minute nap."

He raised one powerful arm above their heads, gripped a low-hanging board, and grinned at her. "Really."

His aftershave reached her senses, but Daisy tried not to drink it in. She took a step backward, but her rear hit the exterior wall of the house.

"What are you doing now?" he asked.

Trying not to fall helplessly for your charms. She cleared her throat. "I'm heading over to the house because I have, uh, lots of laundry to do."

He wrinkled his brow, staring at her.

"Don't give me that look, Jake." She gestured toward her mother's home. "If I go now before it's dark, nobody's going to notice. If they don't notice, they won't report me as an intruder or something.."

He let out a confused laugh, his brows shooting upward. "Laundry will be difficult without electricity."

"Oh! Right ..."

"You can do your laundry here. The set is in the garage and it's all yours."

Daisy's heart felt like it was riding a seesaw—all giggles on the upside and a plummeting stomach on the down. She couldn't let this evening be about small talk or napping, or ... laundry! Anything to take the focus off her, off them. She sighed. Jake was hiding a secret and she wanted to know why. She tilted her chin, snagging him with a look. "Why are you being nice to me all of a sudden? Are you feeling sorry for me or something?"

A grin broke across Jake's face, like an extra-bright beam of sunlight. How did he do that? He stroked her with a gaze, the brush of it sending tingles down her bare arms. "On the contrary, Daisy. You're handling a difficult situation with grit. I've got an army of women behind me and my little project here"—he turned his focus briefly to his family's beach house and back to her again—"while you're tackling everything alone. I have great admiration for you."

She blinked. If only ...

He could see her as more than some kind of warrior.

She could trust him with the deepest thoughts she'd kept locked away.

His admiration could be something ... more.

A large swell of air filled her lungs and Daisy steadied herself. She had to change the subject and do it now. "I heard your phone call, Jake."

His arm dropped from where he casually touched that low board. "My phone call?"

She kept her chin raised. "You're secretly giving Maggie money, right? Why not just tell her?"

Jake's grin melted, first into surprised paralysis, and then slowly into a frown. He licked his lips, the gears of his mind turning right in front of her. "Hmm. Guess I need to learn to lower my voice."

But that would only make it sexier ...

He hung his head now, his eyes imploring her. "What can I say? What you heard is true, but I hope you will help me by keeping it to yourself."

"But she's your sister. At the very least, she would want to know who to thank. I know I would."

"I don't need thanks."

"That's not what I meant."

He shifted. "Look, it's important to me not to take credit, sure. But it's even more imperative that she not be made to feel needy. Does that make sense?"

His words niggled at her. She never really knew the state of her parents' finances. They'd kept those kinds of details from her, as they probably should have. But, at times, she sensed a struggle with lack. Like on those days when she would ask her mother for lunch money and her mother's smile would falter. Or when a shut-off notice would appear on their front door and her father would explain it away as a "clerical error."

Once when she was in the kitchen helping her mother fix "breakfast for dinner," she flipped a pancake and asked, "Momma, are we rich?"

Her mother had kissed her on the cheek and carefully guided her hand away from the hot stove. "We're as rich as we need to be," she'd said.

Jake's brows dipped further, his eyes dark and vulnerable. His often careless, fast-moving banter had suddenly been replaced with a soberness she could not remember ever seeing in him. And her heart toward him softened a little bit more.

She nodded. Maybe she had been thoughtless in her attempt to extract information, to inflict her opinion on his business. She swallowed the taste of pride, her voice a whisper of its former self. "Yes. Of course, I can understand that."

He watched her, no sign of anger or frustration in his face. And then Jake stepped forward, took her into his arms and whispered, "Thank you."

5

Daisy could not stop thinking about the way Jake had touched her last night. It had been innocent, of course. At least in his mind. But in hers, she had given in to the warmth of him, allowing his touch to linger on her skin and in her heart ... for hours.

But she couldn't think of that right now.

A nurse walked into the room where her mother had been living for the past few weeks and made a beeline for her patient. "You almost ready to get out of here, Wren?"

Wren smiled, though there was a slight bit of tilt to her mouth now. "Yes. My Daisy is going to stay with me."

The nurse turned and looked at Daisy, both brows lifted, as if she hadn't noticed her standing there. "What a sweet daughter you are. Do you have a medical background?"

Wren cut in, her voice joyful sounding. "No, no. She builds houses. She's very smart, my Daisy."

Daisy's heart squeezed at the pride in her mother's voice. She had always felt a little guilty for not finishing college, about not being farther along in life—a family, kids—so her mother could have grandchildren running around right about now.

"Good for you," the nurse said to Daisy. She stepped closer, lowering her voice. "It would be a good idea if you spoke to the case manager soon. She'll help you figure out how to best care for your mother's needs once she's out of here."

Daisy nodded at the woman as she left the room. "Thank you. I will."

Wren's eyes sparkled and Daisy wasn't sure she had ever seen her mother look so content. Especially in the years since her father had passed away.

"Take my hand," Wren said.

Daisy curled both of her scraped-up hands around her mother's, hoping she wouldn't notice the abrasions. "You look good, momma."

"I am good. Now that you're here."

Daisy's heart sank a little more. She planned to stay a while, but not forever, though she hadn't exactly planned out how long she would be around this time. "Tomorrow I'm getting your carpets cleaned for you. It's going to smell so fresh inside when you get home." Though she wanted to tell her mother about everything she had done so far on the house, she wasn't sure if doing so would stir up bad memories or even how much she remembered. She still regretted bringing up insurance when her mother was so out of it a couple of weeks back.

Her mother's lips turned downward. "I am so sorry for the mess I left you. Maybe we can paint the wall outside that got a little burned."

Daisy tilted her head and offered her mother a smile. Perhaps it was time to give her some good news after all. She flopped onto the bed and sat beside her mother. "You'll be happy to know that the new siding is almost done."

Her mother gasped. "How?"

"Where do I start?" Daisy settled against her mother's pillow. "For one thing, I hired Rafael to help me with all sorts of things. He's been doing a great job."

Her mother curled her upper lip. "That guy with all the muscles? What sort of things?"

On the one hand, Daisy was encouraged that her mom had the ability to move her lip at all, but on the other, what had brought on that response? And muscles? What?

Daisy gave her head a tiny shake. "Momma, please." She tamped down her gagged laughter.

"I mean it. What is he doing at my house?"

Daisy rubbed her thumb across the soft, translucent skin of her mother's hand. "Well, for one thing, after Jake helped me get the permit, Rafael and I made quick work of the new siding. We're almost done putting it up. We bought it pre-painted, so there's no need to worry about painting it anytime soon. I-I think you'll be super happy when you see it."

She expected her mother to smile, but instead, her expression intensified as if straining to corral scrambled thoughts. "Who is Jake?"

"Holloway. You remember him, don't you?" She did not care to remind her mother that it was Jake's sister, Grace, and her husband, who had literally saved her life. "His family owns the house next to ours?"

Her mother seemed to relax, the stress leaving her face. "Ah, yes. You liked him when you were younger, didn't you?"

Daisy blushed. She could feel the hot flush of it from the tips of her toes to her forehead. Change the subject, change the subject ... "I liked all the Holloway kids. He just happens to be the one in town right now. He's here to give their family home a kitchen makeover."

"Because they are going to sell the house, aren't they?"

The disappointment in her mother's voice was palpable. She didn't like change, that was one of the reasons her own home looked nearly the same way it did when Daisy lived there.

But it was more than that. Wren and Mrs. Holloway had been great friends and her mother missed her. She'd made that clear.

Daisy swallowed, thinking. Truthfully, she felt the same way about their neighbors selling the house. Though she wouldn't likely stay in Colibri Beach forever, the thought of the Holloway family leaving—especially Jake—made a knot form in her throat.

She exhaled and patted her mom's hand. No need to dwell on what-ifs. "Who knows?" She said. "Maybe they're just fixing it up so they can all enjoy it in the summers."

A smile appeared on her mother's face. "Like old times."

"Yes, momma," Daisy said, "like old times.

Daisy stayed awhile longer until her mother's eyelids closed and she fell into easy slumber. Carefully, Daisy slipped out of bed, the news that her mother would soon be released from the rehab center weighing on her. More than anything, she wanted to head home to meet Rafael to finish the job they had started yesterday.

Or maybe what she really wanted was to avoid Jake.

HE'D FELT her all week. Jake had lived alone for years, by choice. His mornings usually consisted of a run and coffee and a bucket full of phone calls. Then work, far into the night. His days had been more or less the same this week, with one exception—though he had not interacted with Daisy much, he had sensed the perfume of her.

Jake charged down the sand later than usual, scattering sandpipers as he ran, the midday sun overhead. Salt-laden oxygen filled his lungs while thoughts of her took over his mind like a Porsche spinning out of control. Purposefully, Jake had left his phone at home. He'd had enough of lawyers and other scoundrels. The foreman on the hotel project remained elusive. A reporter had emailed him during the night, asking for a quote regarding the pending litigation against him. He had respectfully declined comment, then dropped his phone into a drawer and slammed it shut.

Now he began to question that move. Perhaps if he had brought his overactive device with him, his mind would not be so free to obsess over the woman living down the stairs from him.

A gull skittered away from his path, cawing at him, offended. Last night, when Daisy had wandered onto the front porch looking deliciously disheveled, he sensed the sinking of his own ship. The anchor of stability he had dropped when he moved back here last week, the one that told him to do the job and get out, had shifted. The pull between them had been ... unmistakable.

Then she spilled the news that she had been eavesdropping. Jake pumped his arms, jetting a breath from his lungs. In some ways, he was thankful for the detour she had placed in front of him. Just prior to that moment, he sensed that an unpredictable force was about to take over. If she had not asked her questions right then, would there be regret and apology this morning?

He slowed, his house in view, grateful for timely interruptions. The breeze had kicked up a notch, quickly wicking the sweat away from him. Hands on his hips, his breath still pumping, Jake trudged up a sandy embankment toward home.

Jake spotted her standing at the base of her house, looking up, an old-time camera poised in front of her face, that cowboy hat pulled low to her forehead. She looked irresistible with her blonde hair flowing lazily out of that hat.

He followed her line of vision and saw where the lens of her camera was aimed. Rafael was at the highest point of the house, probably inspecting the installation job they'd been working on all week. Jake narrowed his eyes. The guy had forgotten his shirt. Again.

Jake gave his chin a quick shake and turned back toward the sea. Hands at his hips, he slowed his breathing more for a proper cooldown. He had work to do. Plans to draw. Emails to answer. Reporters to fend off. Oh, and a little thing like a kitchen remodel to finish. Jake looked overhead, the light of the day beginning to bounce off the water's surface. He did not have time to wrestle with Daisy ... tempting as the thought might be.

But when Jake turned around, a battle of another kind kicked him in the gut. Rafael had jumped down from that ladder and wrapped his sweaty self around Daisy, leaving her camera to dangle from a strap at her side. The guy was bear-hugging her, staking his claim. Jake's shoulders tensed. He knew he should walk away. Maybe cool down a little longer. Walk the beach. Take some deeper breaths.

Let her go. She's made it clear, jerk, that she's not into you.

Obviously, Daisy was into ... Rafael. The sound of the guy's name in the space of Jake's mind made him want to puke. But what was he supposed to do about it?

He trudged closer to his own house, his eyes focused now on the back door. Learning not to obsess would take some time, but avoidance—that, he could do.

"Jake!"

He turned to see her waving her hat at him, her blonde hair flying in the air. How was he supposed to avoid her now?

Rafael stood closely behind her. Too close, in his opinion.

"Morning," Jake said on approach.

Rafael nodded a hello. On the outside, the guy seemed pleasant enough. But the telltale sign of his true self was that his smile failed to reach his eyes, eyes that continued to assess Jake.

Daisy rose up on her tiptoes. He'd noticed her do this before, and both then and now, it made him want to scoop her up in his arms and carry her across the divide to his house next door.

"We finished installing the siding this morning!" she was saying, snagging his attention again. "What do you think?"

Jake pressed his lips together, reluctantly taking in the work that they had accomplished together. Clean. Professional. Not half bad, though he wished ... what did he wish? That the guy had done a lousy patch-up job that Jake would need to fix? That Daisy had worked outside in the heat putting up siding all by herself?

He forced a smile. "You did a nice job, Daisy."

"Why, thank you very much." She beamed with a certain pride, not the boastful kind. Her face shone with contentment and he noted the way she patted the camera at her waist.

Jake had been surrounded by hard-working women his entire life, but he wasn't sure he had ever seen any of them push quite this hard before. Daisy had tended to her mother's home from dawn to dusk all week long, often toiling alone—except for this latest project. Guilt bubbled inside of him for not having joined her out here to help much.

"Tomorrow I'm having the carpets cleaned and then my mother's things will be delivered next week sometime. Do you think I'll have any trouble getting the city to take down that red tag?"

He shook his head. "Call Mel and let her know that the siding work has been completed. They'll send out an inspector, and if all goes well, he should remove the tag."

"Great." She reached forward and touched his elbow. "Thanks a bunch for the help. I'll go call them now."

He hesitated.

She quirked her head. "Did you have something else to add?"

"Was going to say ... the kitchen remodel is still a few days away from completion. I've been thinking about having a burger all week. Want to grab one with me later tonight?"

Her smile faded and she bit her bottom lip. She glanced

at Rafael. "Oh, we, uh, Rafael and I were planning to celebrate tonight."

"Celebrate?"

"Getting the siding done so quickly." She did that hopping-on-her-toes thing again and her eyes lit. "I know what—come with us. Will you?"

He couldn't think of anything that he wanted to do less. With Daisy in his field of vision, he had imagined he suddenly had time on his hands—that he wasn't actually someone subject to a lawsuit, nor a guy with a half-done kitchen remodel waiting for him. What had he been thinking?

Jake shook his head. "I'll pass. You two enjoy yourselves." He almost choked on the word enjoy.

"Okay, Jake," Daisy said. "See you later tonight."

He nodded once and began to walk toward home. "Yeah. See you."

6

Had she moved too fast? Daisy watched Serge's Carpet Cleaning van pull into the drive with Rafael riding shotgun. As anxious as she was to get the stink out of her mother's old carpets and couch, to prepare for her mother's return home, the siding inspector hadn't made an appearance and she had a niggling feeling that one should have come before the other.

As it stood, she just might find herself in the pickle of having to explain to an inspector why she was allowing two men to roam around the inside of her home with the red tag still firmly in place.

Daisy sighed. She glanced over at Jake's. Yesterday, after finishing up for the day, she and Rafael had walked over to Matty's for pizza only to meet up with a hole-in-the-wall full of old friends. She closed her eyes, unwilling to think about the number of pitchers of beer she had put on her credit card. And she didn't even like beer.

When she returned home, Jake was nowhere to be

found. She knew he was around this morning only by the subtle creaking of floorboards as he moved through the house. By the time she showered and came out here to wait, he seemed to have vanished again.

As Serge hooked up the truck's machine to the hose bib, Rafael opened the house to help clear a path. Soon after, he appeared on the front stoop and waved to Daisy. "Everything is ready for Serge to clean the carpets. He will do the couch too, okay?"

"Great."

He hopped down from the stoop, tromped over to her, and flashed her a bright smile. "Had fun last night. You too?"

"I had a good time too. Thanks again for all the hard work."

He sucked his top lip a moment, watching her. "I let you take me out last night, but next time, it's on me." He brushed her chin with his thumb. "Sound good?"

Daisy opened her mouth, but nothing came out. Rafael laughed. "We can talk about that later. I have a small job two streets away, but I'll return as soon as I'm finished over there. Will you be okay without me over here?"

She closed her mouth and nodded, then watched as Rafael strolled away, humming some unfamiliar tune. Sunlight glinted on his otherwise dark hair. Objectively, she knew he had the ability to melt hearts. She'd seen his swagger, not to mention the rugged abs he never tired of revealing. Daisy exhaled. The thing was, he was still her old friend, Rafael. And she doubted that could ever change.

After he'd gone, a smaller truck arrived and parked right next to Serge's van.

Daisy's lungs clenched. Jon Carnes, the inspector with

the short-cropped hair and dour attitude, marched solemnly toward the house. When he lifted his chin, he did not spare words. "This house has a red tag."

"Yes, I know. Hello again, Jon." She reached out her hand, but he was slow to shake it.

"Shouldn't be letting anyone in there until I've done my inspection."

"I apologize."

"And you should not infer that having an appointment automatically means that the red tag will be removed."

She nodded, her mouth going dry.

His beady eyes watched her unwaveringly from behind thick-framed round spectacles. "Now, show me what's been done."

Daisy led him around the house to the side where the exterior wall had burned. He strode up the steps of the two-story balcony, his expression pinched. From where she stood on the sand, she shaded her eyes with a hand and watched as he leaned close to the newly placed siding, poking it with his hand. "Was waterproofing added underneath?"

"Yes, sir."

"I don't see evidence of it."

She frowned. How could he if it was all covered up? Daisy licked her lips, thinking, but before she came up with an answer, he had already jogged down the steps. "You have the materials?"

"Excuse me?"

He frowned, his cheeks puckering. "The materials used for waterproofing."

"Oh yes, of course—wait." She sighed. "I gave the rest of it to Rafael. He's not here, but I could call and ask him if it's in his truck. Oh!" She shook her head, frazzled. "Never mind. They brought the van today."

He puffed out his lower lip. "You gave your carpet cleaning guy building materials?"

"No, I mean, his brother is the carpet cleaner. Rafael came with him, but then he left for another project. I'm trying to get the house ready for my mother to come home from the hospital. She had a stroke—maybe you know that already—and I really just want it to be perfect ..."

Was she saying too much?

Jon peered at her over those sallow-tinted glasses. "I hope Rafael is a licensed contractor."

She swallowed, thinking. Actually, she wasn't sure, but she should have asked. Chalk that up for one more mistake to add to her list. Daisy's mind raced. What was to happen if she called Rafael to come back and produce his license and he couldn't?

As she worked to hide the fretting going on in her mind, Jake strolled up behind her. She didn't need to turn around to know it was him—she could tell by the sound of his gait, by the way his feet landed in his leather flip-flops.

Jon looked past her. "Hello, Jake."

"What's up, Jon?"

The inspector flipped shut his notepad and stuck it into his front shirt pocket with a pen. "Might have a problem with this siding installation."

Daisy swung a look at Jake, hoping to send him an S.O.S. with her eyes. But he did not return her gaze. Instead, Jake crossed his arms and planted himself right in front of Jon. Her gaze lingered on that familiar move of his.

He stared down the inspector. "Maybe I can help."

Jon stuck out his bottom lip again, like he was looking for trouble. "Daisy here can't prove that waterproofing was installed under all that siding."

Daisy shook her head, cutting in. "What I said was that I gave the extra materials to Rafael. I could always ask him to go home and retrieve them."

"What good would that do?" Jon barked, unfolding his arms. "He might just drive to a hardware store."

Daisy wilted. "I see."

There was no shift in Jake's stance. "C'mon, Jon. You and I both know that waterproofing is important, but not required. But if it helps you check a box, I'll vouch that it was done."

"Sure you wanna go there?" A grin creeped across the inspector's face. "Even after your name's been in the paper about that suspicious project you're mixed up with?"

What was Carnes talking about? Daisy slid a glance at Jake. To his credit, Jake didn't flinch.

"As I said, I'm happy to sign off on Daisy's siding project. I inspected it myself yesterday." He nodded at her. "She did a good job."

Jon clicked his jaw, staring back at Jake. That unnatural grin of his turned to a frown, but he handed him a pen and a form to sign anyway. Once done, Jon shot a look at Daisy. "The red tag is removed. Good luck."

In silence, she and Jake watched Carnes drive away. Daisy quirked a look up at Jake. She wanted to ask the obvious, but didn't. "Thank you for going to bat for me. You've been ... very helpful lately."

Jake unfolded his arms but kept the scowl on his face. His eyes darkened. "I've watched you work your butt off over here getting this house ready for your mother's return." He shook his head, his gaze turning now toward the empty street. "Couldn't let a bully stand in your way."

She nodded. So that was it, the answer to why he had been helping her. She felt a pout forming, but pushed it away. Daisy had much to be thankful for, and she was. Because of Jake's intervention, she could move quickly to finish the repairs of her mother's home and make it livable. More livable than it had been in years. Just knowing her mother would be able to move back in on time gave Daisy such relief.

For some reason, she'd had a difficult time separating the teenage jerk from this kinder adult version of Jake. That had to stop. She might not have won her prince as she had dreamed about as a teen, but he was not the ogre she had made him out to be. At least, not any longer.

Jake dropped his arms to his side. "I've got to get back."

Daisy reached out, her fingers briefly grasping his upper arm. "I'm going to take a walk up to the bakery while Serge is working on the carpets in there. Join me?"

He gave her a confused look, as if not sure what she was asking.

She laughed lightly. "We both have a lot to do, but we need to eat. Besides, I owe you. Come with me?"

Jake's expression softened, and if she wasn't mistaken, he also looked relieved. "Let's do it—but you don't owe me."

She rose up on her toes and wagged a finger in front of his face. "One second while I let Serge know where I'll be."

After she gave Serge her cell phone number, Daisy rejoined Jake outside. Together they made their way down the residential street that led out of their neighborhood, past the little church with the slightly improved appearance, and toward Main Street. When they turned the corner, she pointed to Brooke's Beachside Bakery.

"Must be new," Jake said.

"It is. I found it one day on a walk and fell in love with the place. Well, except ..."

He slowed and quirked a look at her. "Except?"

"Except I ran into Lillian Madsen in there. She tried to get me to list my mother's house."

He opened the door for her. "You're kidding."

As she walked inside, she looked over her shoulder. "I wish!"

The bakery smelled like sugar and yeast with a side of fresh espresso. Daisy breathed it in. Today's quote on the big chalkboard read:

~

Love is like a beautiful flower. ~ Keller

~

SHE TURNED TO JAKE. "What do you think?"

He glanced around, seeming to take it all in, but hesitated before finally saying, "Smells great."

She frowned. "Too pink?"

He peered down at her beneath long lashes. "A little." He laughed. "But don't forget, I grew up in a house of girls. I can take it."

"Hey there, Daisy!" Brooke said. "Lovely to see you again."

"You as well. This is my friend, Jake. He's never been in here."

"Welcome, Jake. Thanks for coming in."

"Pleasure meeting you," he said.

"What can I get you two?"

Daisy turned to Jake.

"Why don't you order for both of us," he said.

"Okay then. We'll have two quiches, two blueberry muffin tops, and two cappuccinos." She looked at Jake. "Do you like oat milk in your espresso."

"Absolutely not."

She laughed and turned back to Brooke. "One of those cappuccinos with oat and the other with cow."

Brooke smiled. "You got it. Grab a table and we'll bring them over to you."

They settled at a table in the corner, away from a window, which suited her just fine. No sense ruining another perfect breakfast with a visit from the town's most notorious real estate agent.

Jake leaned toward her. "You know, I meant what I said. You don't owe me anything. I'm picking up the check."

Daisy's heart skipped a beat. She didn't want Jake to think she was taking advantage of him. "You certainly are not," she replied firmly. "I invited you."

A small smile tugged at the corners of Jake's eyes. "And I'm enjoying spending time with you," he said, his voice low, warm.

Daisy couldn't come up with a retort—she was speechless. She forced herself to stay composed, and not to read any more into those words than what he meant—that he was simply having a nice time.

Although ... he had said *with you*.

She twisted her napkin in her lap and gazed idly around the room. Was it starting to get warm in here?

"Here are your cappuccinos," Brooke said as she approached their table. She put a cup in front of Jake. "This one says 'moo'."

Daisy cracked up.

When Brooke had gone, another woman showed up with their food.

"Muffin tops?" Jake said.

"Of course," Daisy said. "They're the best part, you know."

He nodded, his goofy grin widening. "I believe you."

She took a sip of her cappuccino, lingering on it while gathering her nerve. Finally, she said, "Can I ask you something?"

"Sure. Well, if I can."

"Can ... what?"

He tilted his head. "I, uh, noticed you were taking a picture of Rafael up on that ladder. Are you two ...?

Daisy's laughter crackled in the air between them.

"What did I say?"

She plopped her mouth wide open, searching his face. "Wait ... are you serious? I was shooting a photo of the siding —not Rafael!"

Jake paused, then shrugged. "Could have sworn the guy was posing."

Daisy laughed harder now. "Oh, brother."

He sipped his coffee, a slight grin turning up the corner of his mouth. "What did you want to ask me."

Daisy stared at him for a beat, nearly changing her mind

about her question. She leaned forward, lowering her voice. "What did Jon mean that your name was in the paper? Are you in some kind of trouble?"

The smile Jake had been wearing since the moment that snotty old inspector drove away from her house dissipated. His eyes darkened and he seemed to close up both in word and body language.

She cupped her coffee mug, but didn't drink. Count this as the second time she'd brought up something she shouldn't have. "I apologize. Maybe it was nosy of me to ask."

Jake sighed. "Not really. My firm is involved in litigation that is of public record, so you could easily research it yourself."

"I wouldn't do that."

He snagged her with dark gaze. "But you could if you wanted to."

She eyed him, sensing that a cold drift had taken over. "Forget I said anything."

He reached forward and laid his hand on hers. "I don't want to do this anymore, Daisy."

She tried to pull her hand back, but he intertwined their fingers. She glanced around, hoping others wouldn't notice whatever was happening between them. "I don't understand what you mean," she whispered.

He looked at her fully now, imploring her with a soft gaze. "I know that I'm not your favorite person, that this breakfast is your kind way of saying thanks—though you owe me nothing. But I think ... I know ... that I'm falling for you. And I don't want to act otherwise any longer."

Daisy's heart thudded against the wall of her chest. She made herself look into those brooding eyes of his. Was he teasing? Because if he was, she would never, ever forgive him for this. She realized just how raw and emotional he was capable of making her feel, of how attached she still felt to him after all this time, and how badly this could go if she learned that this was all some kind of joke.

He squeezed her hand. "Say something."

"Are you ... serious?"

Jake's eyes held hers, but he shrank back slightly. He licked his lips. "I want to change your mind about me."

"Jake." She shook her head. "I don't dislike you."

He cracked a smile, albeit a small one. "That's a start."

He caressed her fingers with his, sending a shimmer of headiness through her. He was serious—at least, she thought so. She could feel it in his touch, see it in his gaze. Daisy wanted to believe him, but so many thoughts traversed her mind. Like, why now? Did it have something to do with Rafael's hunky, daily presence? Or was he deflecting from the story that the inspector mentioned? The one about Jake's name being associated with something suspicious?

If she were to lean into something powerful with Jake, only to learn that it was somehow tied to less-than-honest feelings ... she'd be lost.

Jake inhaled and slowly disengaged his hand from hers. He sat back. "Let's start again."

"How?"

"I was going to ask you to tell me about yourself, but first, let me clear the air about what's going on in my life." He crossed his arms onto the table, a look of regret on his face. "I don't want you to have any suspicions of your own about me."

"Stop. I'm embarrassed now. I've been judging you like a

lovesick fifteen-year-old, while you've been nothing but helpful and kind. I'm sorry."

"Lovesick, huh?"

"Jake!"

He chuckled. "How do you do that?"

"What?"

"Pull me out of my funk so fast." He grabbed her hand again and wrapped both of his around it. "I need you in my life, Daisy."

This time, when she looked into his wanting eyes, felt the strong embrace of his hands around hers, she knew he meant it.

What she didn't know was if a relationship between her and Jake could actually survive.

AFTER BREAKFAST, they walked back to Daisy's house. Even with a rise in the day's humidity, her conversation at the bakery with Jake had made her feel as if she was floating on a sea breeze—despite the problem he faced in Los Angeles. Though she didn't know all the details, Jake's setback fed a desire within her to help him as he had helped her, though she had no idea how.

When they returned, Serge was outside of his van, reassembling the parts of the cleaning machine. She sensed movement near the house and looked up to find Rafael standing on the stoop, watching them, his thick arms crossed across his bare chest.

Daisy turned to Jake. "I need to take care of paying Serge. Talk later?"

He grinned and reached out to play with a tendril of her wayward hair. "You bet. Let me take you to dinner tonight."

"Tonight?"

He raised one brow. "Tell me you haven't made plans with that pretty boy again."

She grabbed his hand from where it played with her hair. "Jake," she hissed. "Shush or he'll hear you."

Jake slid a glance toward the front door of her house. "Maybe I need to speak a little louder then."

Daisy continued to whisper harshly, a laugh playing on her face. "You're ridiculous. Yes, I'll have dinner with you. Now, go."

He chuckled and kissed her hand before she broke free of him. As he was walking backward across the divide to his family's house, he called back, "And wear those stilettos!"

Daisy stole a quick glance back at him before returning her attention to Serge, who had just closed up the door to his van. She hoped her face didn't look as red as it felt. "All finished?"

"I am. Got a lot of dirt and smoke out of there. You'll need to stay off of the carpets at least a day, especially with this muggy weather we're suddenly having."

So she wouldn't be able to move back into her mother's house quite so fast ... she tried to hide her smile. "Got it. Can I text payment to you tonight?"

"Sure thing," Serge said.

Rafael leaned his arms onto the railing near her front door. "You have accomplished much in one day, Daisy."

She looked up, shading her eyes with a hand. He wore an expression she couldn't read. "You heard then ... about the red tag being removed?" She didn't mention how close she was to failing inspection and Rafael's potential part in that.

He shrugged and darted a glance toward Jake's. "I figured as much."

"Such good news, right?"

He didn't answer right away. Instead, he pushed himself off the railing and raised both palms. "Yes. Excellent news. But what's going on with you and Jake?"

She stepped closer to the stoop. "We're friends."

Rafael gave her a closed-mouth humph. "Thought he was dead to you."

Daisy winced. "Did I say that?"

"Yes. You acted like it, too."

"I shouldn't have done that."

He crossed his arms. "So you and that guy are a thing now?"

Daisy shrugged, though her mouth curled into a smile on its own volition. "Not a thing, but we have, uh, laid down our weapons, so to speak."

Rafael groaned. He pulled his T-shirt out of his back pocket and slid it over his head and down his chest. "I'm happy for you, Daisy. I am." He waved to his brother to wait for him.

The frost coming off of Rafael made her fingers grow cold. She felt caught between the friendship of their youth and the expectations that came with adulthood. She dipped her chin, watching the tension in the way he moved, the way he averted his eyes from hers. "Will you be back, Rafael?"

Suddenly, he leaned in close to her, his voice deep, heavy. He looked her in the eye. "My work here is done. If you need anything, I'm sure your neighbor can handle it."

She froze as he hopped down to the sand, jogged over to Serge's van, and jumped inside. Daisy watched them ramble away, leaving her to relive the past few weeks. Had she somehow led Rafael to think she felt more for him than friendship? Had he given her any sign that he wanted something more?

Next time, it's on me.

Rafael's words about going out with him again breezed through her mind. She'd been a little caught off guard earlier today by his uncharacteristic intimacy, but really, she hadn't thought all that much about it. Maybe that was because she hadn't felt anything more than friendship for him.

Daisy blew out a long, slow breath, her gaze steady on the empty road. She'd had dozens of dates, but no serious boyfriend all of these years. Her inability to read men's minds probably had something to do with that.

When she turned back toward the house, another reality hit her. She still had much to do to prepare for her mother's return. On the stoop, she peered inside the house and breathed in that chemically laden scent emanating from the freshly washed carpet. So much better than all that smoke from the fire and her mother's occasional cigars.

Daisy slipped out of her shoes and into the house. She tip-toed around, noting how careful Serge had been with her mother's things. Couch cushions were standing on end to dry against the wall and foam cups had been placed under furniture feet. For the first time since she'd been back, she could squint and just about make out the finish line.

7

W hy had he agreed to this? It had been a certain form of excruciation having Daisy live under the same roof with him, feeling the way he did.

You're a grown man. Suck it up.

Sunday had come. He gulped his coffee and stared out across the divide between their two houses. The fog had rolled in, giving the day a gray and ominous feel. He huffed. His mother loved days like this. She saw color in the gray, not darkness as he always had. He felt her loss painfully on days like today, which might be the reason for his sullen mood.

Or maybe it was the slow drip of a reminder of something else that burdened him. Wren Mcafee would be coming home soon—as in, next week. He downed his coffee, mulling on that fact. At the same time, Maggie's admonishment rang in his ears. His sister had told him to let the matter of her relationship with his father go, and though he found that he still harbored some resentment, he also felt dutifully ashamed.

But should he be?

What kind of son would he be not to care if his father had taken up with the neighbor woman when his mother was too ill to notice? Then again, what chance did he have with Daisy if he were to cling to his suspicions? She had burrowed her way deep into his psyche. He wanted to know so much more about her. Where had she been the past ten years? What had she seen and done? Why all the cowboy hats?

Jake shook his head, a grunt of a sigh leaving him. His emotions had been an overactive slingshot lately, shooting every which way, and he wasn't used to it. Nor did he like it.

From a young age, he knew what he wanted: success. He promised himself to get his architecture degree and build amazing structures to make the world stop and admire. He'd done that—and had become quite successful at it. It hadn't hurt, though, that he had invested his first five-thousand-dollar profit in Netflix. He'd weathered their downturn and stayed invested, only to see an eventual three-hundred-plus-percent return. He had been investing ever since, using the money to grow his own company.

A billion dollars. That's how much he was worth in dollars. Enough to buy this old beach house from his parents' estate and hand it back to his siblings mortgage-free. But their will stipulated that they each must live in it for a month. Work on it themselves. And do it all on a budget.

And if they did not comply? The house, like all of their other assets, would be given to charity. The will's executor would make sure that happened. He whistled and shook his head. Asking his parents why would be one of the first questions he uttered when his sorry self landed in heaven.

Speaking of heaven, a little slice of it just bounded down the steps of the Mcafee house wearing cut-off denim shorts, a bare midriff tee, and ... a cowboy hat. Mercy. Suddenly the gray day brightened. He swung open the door and called out to her. "Coffee break?"

Daisy stopped. She was carrying a paint roller, a tray, and one weary smile. Just how long had she been over there painting?

"That's music to my ears, Jake. I'll be right over."

He shook his head. "Give me a minute and I'll come to you."

Quickly, Jake poured a mug of coffee, adding some oat milk to it—even though that was pure madness—and put it on the island while he refilled his own mug and added cream. He found her outside cleaning the roller and pan in a bucket, her hands stained with paint. She grabbed the mug anyway and took a long sip. "So good. Thank you."

He chuckled. "You're welcome. How long you been up?"

She sighed. "Since five. Couldn't sleep so I thought I'd come over and prep for more painting. I started as soon as daylight showed its face."

"Hmm. How about a break and then I help you out? If we work together, we could probably slam out the rest of the painting by day's end."

She peeked at him over a sip of coffee. "That's really nice of you."

He took the coffee mug from her and set it on a step.

She gasped. "Now? Can't I take my coffee with me?"

"In a minute." He encircled her waist with his arms and

cinched her closer. She smelled like citrus ... with a dollop of paint mixed in.

She lifted her chin, staring at him. "What're you smiling about?"

"Was just thinking about The Wizard of Oz."

"What? Why?"

He grinned, closing the space between them.

She gasped and yanked herself away from him. "Munchkin! You were smiling because you're thinking of calling me munchkin again!"

"Shh." He cupped her face with his hand. "I'm trying to kiss you."

Her eyes flashed. Her chin lifted even higher. "Oh, yeah?"

"Yeah."

"You're gonna have to apologize first."

He tilted his head, trying to figure her out, then chuckled as he did. "I'm sincerely sorry."

She moved closer whispering, "Liar." Then didn't wait, but closed the space between them, and kissed him so quickly, so sweetly, he thought he'd lose his mind. She'd been here all along, but suddenly, all Jake could think was, *where has Daisy been all my life?*

DAISY HAD ALWAYS IMAGINED that kissing Jake Holloway would be like one never-ending firework show. That his touch would sear her with a passion that even her dreams could not conjure up. And that she would be forever changed—and spoiled—by the press of his lips against hers, and never even think about another boy again.

She had not been wrong. Nor disappointed—even though she was the one to close the deal.

The only question now was whether she could ever think about another guy again. Daisy considered this as she cleared away a tarp from her mother's kitchen and inspected the paint job. She had chosen a soft yellow for the walls to counteract the often-gray weather that living on the coast brought with it. Her mother had always loved lavender and yellow together, so Daisy planned to cut some sprigs of lavender from her mom's garden, plop them into vases, and place them around the kitchen.

Her mind wandered back to Jake, her heart doing a strange little flip at the thought of him, like she was a teen again and Jake had just emerged from his parents' house with beach towel over his shoulder and a surfboard under his arm. After he brought her coffee and she surprised herself by kissing him—she kissed Jake Holloway!— he helped her paint, as promised. They talked about everything and nothing all at the same time. And, reluctantly, he retreated to his family's beach house soon after to work on his own kitchen remodel.

How would she ever keep her mind on all that she still had left to do?

Daisy exhaled and evaluated the living room. She put the couch cushions back in their spot and arranged her mother's pillows as if she were preparing for a photo shoot in a home magazine.

Next, she found the pictures she had removed from the walls and laid them on the kitchen floor. She had been tempted to buy some inexpensive wall art, but changed her mind. In the end, Daisy wanted her mom to feel the comfort and familiarity of home. So instead she rearranged them in a way that she hoped would make the house feel spruced up —but not like a different home. She also added several of the shots she'd taken with her own camera.

For the next hour, she re-hung all pictures and artwork throughout the living room and kitchen in a fresh way. She also put away clutter and chose a few personal items to decorate the tabletop, credenza, and bookshelves.

She'd been so absorbed in her redesign of the room that she barely noticed the screen door opening. Jake entered the house, a goofy grin on his face.

"Hey." His eyes brushed over hers before he turned to admire the room. Jake let out an appraising whistle. "Wow. It's like a new place in here."

"I hope my mom loves it. I didn't buy anything new. Just rearranged what she had. Oh, except for the photos I took of the little church near here. Sorry, none of Rafael."

Jake groaned, and Daisy laughed in response.

"I'll ignore that remark," he said. "But the chapel photos are amazing. You used black and white film."

She nodded. "That's something I've been playing around with, yes. Fortunately, I found a place in town that could develop it for me."

He moved closer to view one photo—the little church highlighted by the sun's face shining on it, the backdrop in the shadows. "The contrast really draws the eye to the place."

"Hmm," she said. "I remember how full that church seemed whenever your family came to town."

He seemed to turn that thought over in his mind, a quiet smile on his face. Eventually, Jake turned his gaze the living room, sweeping a look from one corner to another. "Have you ever thought of becoming a home stager? If you hadn't told me that you had reused what was already here, plus a few of your own additions, I wouldn't have guessed." Jake slid an arm around her waist. "Impressive job."

"Glad you think so." She noticed Jake's eyes landed on a set of sea star sculptures with a stack of postcards between them. "Those are postcards that I sent to my mom over the years from all the places I've traveled. I found them in a drawer with a rubber band around them, so I thought it would be fun to display them. It really touched me to learn that she kept them."

Quietly, Jake walked forward and touched the stack, pulling out one of the cards randomly. He flipped it over to the picture of a beach the color of sea glass. Daisy laughed. "Of all the places I've gone, that's probably the closest. It's a beach just south of Monterey."

"Mexico?"

She shook her head, smiling. "California."

He nodded and slid the postcard back into that stack.

"So," she said, noticing the pensive look on his face, "I didn't expect to see you so soon today."

He gave her a small smile, that sober expression gone. "Oh, really."

"Not that I'm not thrilled to see you, of course."

He turned her around until they were face-to-face and smoothed her hair back with one stroke of his hand. "Of course."

Her voice became a whisper. "Because I am, you know."

"Thrilled to see me?"

"Mm-hm." She leaned into him, her temple leaning

against his chest until she could hear the beating of his heart.

"I'm glad you're thrilled," he said. He lifted her chin with the crook of his finger and kissed her softly, sending the fluttering of butterfly wings through her. Just in case she'd doubted his response to her kiss from earlier, she needn't have worried. "I have to get back to work, but I just wanted to do that."

For the second time in a day, Daisy wondered how she could fully commit her attention to the tasks in front of her. She swallowed a sigh and curled up on the couch. How long had it been since a guy left her feeling all swoon-y like this?

Truthfully? Never. Well, unless she counted the years she pined after Jake in those summers when he was home and ignorant of her presence. All she wanted to do for the rest of the day was wrap a soft blanket around her body and daydream.

She glanced around and realized—no blanket in sight. Daisy pulled herself back up and padded down the hall with great effort. She searched her mother's linen closet remembering the blankets she'd washed after arriving in Colibri a few weeks ago. Her fingers landed on soft fabric. Daisy pulled the woven cotton throw from the back of the closet and brought it to the couch. She draped it over the side of one arm of the couch. There. Now she could daydream about Jake while wrapped in a blanket anytime she wanted.

She glanced out the window toward Jake's house. Though he had bounded over here with a certain enthusiasm, she had noticed a tinge of melancholy after he'd come. She hadn't wanted to acknowledge it, given what had transpired between them, but even after the kiss, he seemed ...

preoccupied. Jake hadn't mentioned much about the troubles he was facing in LA, and she didn't want to pry, but maybe the stress of it all was weighing on him.

Daisy's cell phone rang, interrupting her thoughts about Jake. "This is Daisy."

"Hello, Ms. Mcafee. This is Lynette, your mother's nurse?"

Daisy straightened, alert to the reality of why she was here in the first place. "Yes. Hi."

"Your mother asked me to dial the phone for her. She'd like to speak to you. Is now a good time?"

"Always. Yes. Please put her on."

The phone shuffled and shifted in her ear until her mother's thin voice came on the line. "Hello?"

Daisy frowned. She sounded weak, maybe even a little afraid. "Momma, it's Daisy. Are you okay?"

"Oh Daisy! It is you."

She laughed lightly, her mother's response endearing. "Were you expecting someone else?"

"No, dear. I was wondering, though, if you could do me a favor?"

"Of course. What is it?"

"I'd like you to take some cuttings of my lavender bushes to the Holloway house. Grace loved that I brought her some —you know their mother loved my lavender plants, too. Would you take some to Jake, darling? You can wrap them in newspaper ... oh dear, I suppose all the newspaper is gone from the house now."

Daisy grinned. Her mother wanted Daisy to take Jake some flowers, a sure sign she was getting her strength back. "I'd be happy to do that, Mom. Don't worry about the newspaper—I'll wrap them in paper towels. Now you get some rest. Pretty soon they'll let me take you home, but you have to be strong enough, okay?"

"Okay, dear. Bye-bye."

Daisy hung up, fresh happiness washing through her. She'd never felt so alone as when she learned about her mother's stroke. Even with all of her travels, her mother had only been a phone call away. She stilled, thinking about where her life might take her next, knowing the relief organization she worked for didn't have any projects near Colibri Beach.

She sighed, determined not to think about the future right now. Instead, Daisy wandered outside, grabbed a bucket, and clipped some of the healthiest stalks of lavender that she could find.

8

B y the time late afternoon rolled around, Daisy was ready to grab that super soft blanket from her mother's couch and roll herself right inside of it. The only thing that would make that scenario better was if Jake would join her.

She peered outside. Lights blazed from inside his house, indicating that he was still at it. A delivery truck from one of the local appliance stores pulled up a few hours ago and a couple of guys had wheeled some pretty large boxes into the garage. She would have gone over to investigate, but she'd found herself slapping a fresh coat of white paint onto her mother's bathroom walls. She couldn't help herself. When she had opened up the room to get it ready for her mother's return, she was taken aback by how dingy it had become.

How could she let that go?

She couldn't. So she spent the afternoon painting, cleaning up after herself, and grabbing a quick shower. Her pantry was still empty—she was still staying with Jake, after all. So she made a quick trip to the store, grabbed a couple of steaks, a bag salad, and a bottle of red wine, and brought them all over to Jake's along with everything else they'd need.

He answered the door with a quick smile and an even quicker kiss on her lips. He smelled good, like a man who had been working hard all day. "You don't have to knock, you know."

Daisy shrugged and stepped inside with her bag of groceries and accompaniments. Technically, she was still staying with him—though that would change very soon— but given the shift in their relationship, she wasn't sure of the protocol. Or was that overthinking things?

"What have you got there?" He peered into the bag, his eyes quickly finding hers again.

She slid the bag onto the new island and turned around to face him. Vaguely she noticed shiny appliances that had yet to be hooked up. "Thought I'd grill these steaks. Okay if I use your barbecue?"

He moved closer to her, a sly grin on his lips. Any closer and he'd have her pinned against the island. Her palms found his chest and rested there.

He tipped up her chin, the grin still on his face. "Unless, of course, you're not hungry," she said, her cheeks warming.

He bent his face close to hers. "Oh, I'm hungry ... really hungry."

Daisy laughed lightly at this. She wadded up the fabric of his tee with one hand and rose up on her tiptoes, leaning into his kiss, the effect of it causing her body to simultaneously weaken and gain strength. He pulled back only to kiss her again with even more fire than before. When they parted, she stared up at him, disoriented. "Um, so the steaks?"

He chuckled and took one of her hands, kissing it before walking her to the back door that led outside to the deck. "I'm starved. I'll clean myself up and meet you back here soon. Want to eat out here?"

She nodded. "Yes. Perfect." He went back inside and she glanced out to the sea. The haze of the day had blown inland just in time for the sun to provide its nightly entertainment. Its descent had already begun, blazing up the sky in scores of red, orange, and a dash of pink. She'd seen this many times as a kid, but had she appreciated it the way she did now?

Daisy fired up the propane and let it warm the grill. She opened the wine to let it breathe and tossed the salad in the ceramic bowl she had brought with her.

When the grill sizzled, she salt-and-peppered the steaks and set them over the flame. The aroma brought back memories, particularly of her father who always preferred being outdoors to staying inside the house. He'd often come home from work, search around the house for her, and prod her to join him on a walk to the water. "Gotta get some salt air in you, Daisy," she remembered him saying. "It's good for the soul."

Maybe that's why she chose to work for a relief agency that focused on coastal areas. Not that she spent all that much idle time at the beach, like she had when she was growing up. Her parents had always taught her the value of hard work, of praying for direction, and accomplishing something by the end of each day. She had carried those rules-to-live-by with her into every project, thankful that her father had left her some money to fall back on—if she ever needed it.

Jake joined her outside wearing a fresh T-shirt and shorts, his dark hair looking towel dried. He held two wineglasses in one hand. "What'd I miss?"

"Your timing is perfect because these bad boys are ready." She plated two medium-well steaks and put them on the table.

"Such service," he said, pouring them each a glass of wine. He handed one to her. "Cheers."

They sat next to each other at the wooden table that had probably been in this same spot for decades, their plates full, the watercolor sky showing off before them. "God's artistry never gets old."

Jake swallowed, then swung a look out to the horizon. "I'll say. Sometimes I forget that."

"Because you never slow down enough."

He turned to acknowledge her. "You know me too well." He paused. "Being here, though, is a reminder of his creativity. No matter how hard I try, I'll never be able to accomplish anything that compares with all that beauty."

She was quiet for a moment as they sat next to each other, admiring the view. "And yet, every creative thing you've done is a reflection of God in you."

A slow smile made its way across his face, the comfortable quiet between them continuing as they ate their dinner. Eventually, he said, "This steak is perfect. Have you always been such a great cook?"

She laughed. "Um, I grilled steak and opened a bag salad. I'd hardly call that the method of a great cook."

"Don't underestimate yourself." He swallowed another

bite and washed it down with a sip of the wine. He leveled his gaze on her. "Was I really a jerk to you when we were kids? I mean, other than that time I turned down your invitation to the dance."

"And the castle versus ranch house incident."

He frowned. "Oooh."

"Yeah, you kind of were." She laughed and shrugged. "I can't really blame you. Not anymore, at least."

"Oh no?"

"One thing I recall about you as a teenager is how fast you moved." She paused, sipping her wine and looking out to sea, remembering. "I always thought you were just, I don't know, ignoring me on purpose. And maybe you were at times."

He groaned. "I wasn't."

"Okay." She smiled at him. "But really, now that I see how quickly your mind moves, how you always seem to have something to occupy it—and how successful you have apparently become—I'm realizing that what I interpreted as willful evasion was probably you just being you."

He winced. "Ouch."

Daisy laughed. "That wasn't meant to be an insult. What I'm saying is that you were probably thinking about all you were going to do with your life, about your future. I was a kid with a big crush." She gave him a shy smile. "I understand now that it wasn't personal."

The sun, golden orange, hung over the sea. With the crashing of waves in the background, Jake slid closer to her, their conversation quieting as they set down their forks and stared at the horizon. As a kid, she too had many goals, though most of them revolved around her ability to shape wet sand into something magnificent. But there was something even more perfect about a moment like this, where beauty and silence entwined with one another to draw two people close. Beneath the old wooden table, Jake's hand, warm and strong, found hers. Together they watched the day sink into the sea, the glow of it shooting its swan song into the night sky.

"I'm sorry that I ignored you back then." He squeezed her hand. "Don't deny that I did. Forgive me?"

She whispered, "I already have."

Then, a catch in her throat reminded her of the little girl who sat on that great big expanse of sand out there, hoping her prince would arrive and, well, at least notice her. Daisy smiled knowing that he finally had.

THE NEXT DAY, Jake hoped his sisters wouldn't notice just how fine the lines of the new cabinets were. Nor did he care for them to figure out the retail cost of the upgraded stainless steel appliances that now outfitted the beach house kitchen. He had made the purchases with a brief phone call to a vendor he worked with often, charged them to his business account, and quickly painted the space while waiting for everything to arrive.

Now that the room looked more like the kitchen it would eventually be, he wondered if his sisters would question his choices. Daisy, for her part, had swooned when she saw how the new space had emerged. Though it was still a work in progress, even he had been pleased with the results. Jake had not built anything with his own hands in years. The peaceful sense of accomplishment that working on this project brought surprised even him.

A rapid knock on his door pulled Jake out of his reverie. He traversed the space and opened the door.

"Well, hello there, Jake!" Lillian Madsen stood on the porch, tiger-eye sunglasses framing her eyes. She reached a hand out to him, her voice suddenly turning sympathetic. "How are you, dear?"

Jake wiped a hand on his jeans before shaking her hand. "I'm well, Lillian. Can I help you?" He didn't care to waste time having small talk with the town busybody.

"Cut to the quick, okay. I understand. Well." She swung a look around, briefly landing her gaze on the Mcafee's house. "I'm looking for Daisy. Have you seen her lately?"

Jake resisted the urge to close the door to a sliver-sized opening. As a matter of fact, he had seen the beautiful Daisy Mcafee today. She was taking a well-deserved siesta—he'd practically forced her to lay down after she had the idea to paint yet another couple of rooms at her mother's house. He wasn't about to let old sell-em-while-the-body's-still-warm Madsen disrupt her.

"Haven't seen her in a while, but if there's a message, I can pass it along when I do."

Something stirred behind him and he turned. "Jake?"

Daisy's hair looked deliciously disheveled. He took in her cut-offs, short tee, and bare feet and bit back a swear. He'd been trying to protect her, but really, he didn't care to share the gorgeous, half-asleep woman in his house with Madsen.

Lillian gasped. "Oh there she is," she said, her voice in mock surprise. "How perfect that you are already here. Now Jake won't have to play messenger for me."

Daisy rubbed a hand over her face, reality dawning. She stepped closer to the front door, though Jake had made no effort to invite the visitor in. "Hey, Lillian," Daisy said, stifling a yawn.

"Oh my. Have I disturbed you two?" The woman's crayon-red lips uncoiled into a smile that would make the Joker jealous. "Would you like to, perhaps, get dressed before we meet?"

Daisy frowned, tilting her head to the side. "Excuse me, Lillian, but I think there's a mistake. I-I'm not aware of any meeting."

"Well, I will have to get back to my office and fire my scheduler." Lillian tsked and sighed, not looking surprised at all. "I apologize for the oversight but I really must speak to you today."

Jake cut in. "What is this about?"

Lillian shrank back with a flare. She moved her dramatic wide-eyed gaze from Jake to Daisy. "This is a private matter between my client and myself, Jake. Unless, of course, Daisy would not mind if I spoke about it for both of you to hear?"

Daisy put her hand on Jake's shoulder, suddenly looking fully awake. "I've got this," she said, commandeering the door. She crossed her arms. "Just tell me what it is, Lillian. You can say it in front of Jake."

Her face lit up. "Well, I have got an offer for your mother's home!" She held up a folder with the logo of Madsen Real Estate & Investments emblazoned across it. "All cash, dear, so you will want to move very quickly on this. I can't say for certain how long these buyers will wait for a decision."

Jake grabbed the door. "Are you out of your mind?"

"I beg your pardon? Tsk, tsk." The woman shook her head, her comical lips pursed. "Jake Holloway, if your lovely parents could hear you now!"

"You listen to me, Ms. Madsen," Daisy said. "I already told you that my mother's home is NOT for sale. She will be coming home very soon and I don't want her to hear any of this nonsense from you, and I certainly don't want to hear anymore of it myself either."

"But—"

"She will be staying in her home for the foreseeable future. Do you understand me?"

Lillian shut her mouth. She blinked, her expression freezing in place, as if thoroughly insulted. Daisy didn't need him to save her. Not at all. He swiveled his chin enough for Daisy, alone, to see the spark in his eyes. He saw the same expression pass through hers, though she did an admirable job of keeping it stern for Lillian's sake.

"Now," Daisy said, her hand on the door, "it's time for you to leave. I have a boyfriend to kiss."

She shut the door but not before Lillian curled her lip and let out a dramatic gasp.

Jake threw back his head, laughing to the rafters. He pulled Daisy into his arms, lifting her off her feet. "That was amazing." He went in for a kiss, but she turned her head and his mouth landed on her cheek. "Hey!"

She gave him a guilty grin. "Sorry. Morning breath."

"Come here." He cinched her closer, kissing her on the mouth despite her squeals of protest.

When he put her down, she sighed. "Oh that woman is going to drive me crazy."

"Yeah, well, she drove my parents nuts. The only reason

she is going after you instead of me is that she knows we're not able to sell this place. At least not yet." Almost immediately, Jake regretted his words as they brought uncertainty into the light. He only had another ten days at this house, and then what? And what about Daisy's job with the relief organization? She had told him early on that, after her mother was settled safely back into her home, she would be leaving again to save the world.

He considered the woman in his arms, her embrace quickly becoming an indelible memory that he wanted to revisit again and again. "You hungry?" he asked.

Daisy sighed. "A little. But I still have some painting to finish up."

He kissed her head. "I know. But I just filled up my brand-new fridge, so you have to help me eat everything."

Daisy laughed. "Well, I do like to help out those in need. Let me go wash up and—"

"What's he doing here?" The crackling of truck tires nearby had caught Jake's attention and he leaned to look out the window between their houses. Rafael had driven up to Wren's place and parked.

Daisy came up behind him. "No idea." She kissed his cheek. "I'll go find out. Make me a delicious sandwich to have when I get back?"

Jake hesitated. He'd rather be her bodyguard when she was talking to the shirtless wonder over there, but was it his place? He slid a glance at her as she stepped into the flip-flops she had left by his front door. "You're sure you don't want me to ...?"

She swung a questioning look over her shoulder, her brows scrunched. "To what?"

He hadn't exactly earned the right to give her his opinion about her choices, let alone dissuade her from making them. Still, it took mighty willpower to keep his thoughts to himself. "Never mind," he finally said. "But hurry back. I don't want you fainting from hunger while you're there."

Her smile turned whimsical. "Gotchyou. Be back in a flash."

~

A HEAVY BREEZE pitted Daisy's bare legs with sand particles as she walked over to where Rafael stood on her porch. He turned and flashed that bright smile on her as she ascended the steps to the door, but it dissipated when his gaze wandered to Jake's place, from where she had come.

"Hey, Rafael."

He nodded. "Daisy."

"Want to see all the work that I've accomplished this past week?" She didn't care to hold a grudge, to be angry with him for not sticking around to help her with all the projects she had intended for him.

"I just came to pick up some tools that I left behind."

"Hmm. Okay." She turned away from the door. "I think they're mostly in the garage. Can you follow me?"

They took the steps down from the deck and walked around the front of the house to the garage. Daisy bent to lift the door to the garage, but Rafael wordlessly reached for the handle and opened the door himself. They had been friends for as long as she could remember and his silence pained her.

Rafael walked toward the tools he had left piled up on

her father's workbench, but she reached out and grabbed hold of his arm. He twisted, looking first at where her hand gripped him, and then at her.

"Hey," she said, tilting her head to one side.

He shrugged her off and began shoving tools into the belt he'd brought with him. "I'll just take my tools and get out so you can go back to ... whatever you were doing."

"Rafael, what's wrong? You and I have been friends for a long time. Why are you mad at me?"

His eyes flashed when he faced her, an exasperated half-smile on his face. "I'm not mad. Never at you, Daisy."

"Then why the cold shoulder?"

He licked his bottom lip. "What can I say? I don't like to be beat." He spat out a sigh. "Should have known you'd pick the rich guy over a lowly handyman. They all do, you know?"

Daisy pressed a hand into the side of her waist. "First of all, he's not rich." She didn't know this for sure, but didn't care either. "And second, there's nothing lowly about you at all. Shoot, Rafael, I remember how all the girls fawned over you in high school. So nauseating!"

He puckered his mouth, nodding, a grimace forming. "So where are they all now?"

"Maybe you've become more selective than you were back then."

"You're right," he said, his voice thick. "I am."

His eyes snagged with hers and Daisy had never felt this awkward with him. Ever. A thought crept into her consciousness. Had she noticed the feelings he had, apparently, been forming for her? Or had he been invisible to her, as she was to Jake way back when?

"Rafael, I'm sorry if I ... that I didn't notice or understand ..."

He draped his full tool belt over one shoulder. "Don't sweat it, Daisy girl. I know I won't."

Before she could add a thing, he stalked out of the garage and out of sight. What in the world? Two men in one month ... a record for her, for sure.

Daisy shut the garage door and wandered back into the kitchen at Jake's place where a tempting sandwich waited for her. She sighed, washed her hands, and took the plate over to the dining room table. Her stomach tumbled just as Jake came around the corner to hand her a can of Perrier. "Want to talk about it?"

"I guess I hurt his feelings." She swallowed a bite of sandwich, holding back part of what Rafael said—particularly the comment about Jake's financial status. "I hate that."

"Something tells me that guy has broken a few hearts in his lifetime."

"Oh, so you're into him now?"

He choked. "Are you kidding me?"

Daisy giggled. "Yeah, I am."

Jake wagged his head, chuckling. "My guess is he hasn't worried too much about the pixie dust he's trampled along the way. He'll survive."

"Hmm." She ate her sandwich, considering him. When she finished another bite, she said, "Like you have?"

He lowered his brows. "Believe me, I haven't had a whole lot of time to date, let alone feel the full effects of the breakup of a long-term relationship."

She slid her gaze to her sandwich, reality hitting her. *I hope you never will, Jake, I hope you never will.*

Jake flashed her a smile and reached over to hold her hand. "You, on the other hand, have turned out to be quite the heartbreaker!"

"What does that mean?"

"Hey, Romeo over there was pulling out all the stops for you, but you pretty much said, 'Naw, pretty boy. Keep that shirt on because I'm not into you.'"

"Oh my gosh, I did not." She laughed. "You're crazy, Jake."

He stood and reached for her hand. "Let's play hooky and go to the beach."

Daisy bit her lip. The downstairs bathroom was covered in plastic and blue tape. She still needed to put switch plates and outlet covers back in place. But Jake's puppy dog gaze was too much. She had hoped for a moment like this for years, so why turn it down in favor of her to-do list?

She nodded. "I'd love—"

Jake's cell phone disrupted the room. "Sorry. Hang on while I get that." He retrieved it from the kitchen. "This is Jake."

As he listened to the caller, Jake began to pace, punctuating the silence occasionally with one- or two-word answers or grunts. "Yes." Groan. "Got it. Absolutely. Let me know."

Daisy threw out her paper plate and returned to wipe down the dining room table. She kept herself busy, concerned by the seriousness in Jake's tone, yet not feeling comfortable enough to ask him for details about the fines and possible litigation he faced. She chased away a niggle of thought that she might just be a distraction for Jake during a stressful time. Daisy shook her head physically, unwilling to allow herself to go there. Not now. Not after the way he'd kissed her today. And the day before. And the day before that.

Jake signed off on his call and shoved his phone into his pocket. Without missing a beat—and without a word concerning the content of his phone call—he turned to Daisy and said, "Let's go."

They wandered out to the beach, hand-in-hand, their feet bare. In some ways, she felt more like a teenager now than ever. Despite the call Jake had taken a few minutes ago, the wide-open expanse of sand that led to the sea had the ability to throw open the door to infinite possibilities. She had forgotten how life at the beach had made her feel, had taken the quiet, sometimes monotonous days for granted, when she should have been pining for them as much as she had for Jake.

The tide was out, giving them a long, flat beach to walk. Quickly, their strides fell into sync. Jake turned to her. "My call with my sisters will be tonight."

Daisy nodded. "Okay. I'll be at Mom's place touching up a few things. Call me when you're done?"

He squeezed her hand. "Stay. They'll want to say hi. And to make sure I haven't locked you out of the house or something."

"Like you used to do to them."

He chuckled. "What can I say? They were brats."

Daisy laughed and grabbed his arm with her free hand. "Actually, there's a lot I want to ask them, so yes, I will accept your invitation to stay in the house tonight while you are on the phone with your sisters."

Jake groaned. "On second thought, maybe you would be more comfortable at your mother's."

"You mean since there's actually no electricity yet? Of course, I could curl up under a few blankets. Sure, that would be no prob—"

He wrapped both arms around her and lifted her into the air, her squeals competing with the roll of the surf. "Put me down, Jake Holloway!"

He laughed. "You like saying my name, don't you?"

Daisy liked everything about him and it scared her to bits. She wasn't ready to confess that to him, though. Not yet. "Well, all I can say is that I remember your momma standing out on that back porch, calling you into dinner."

"Oh, so you're trying to mother me. I see."

"I'm just trying to get your attention."

He stopped and pulled her toward him then, his hot breath inches from her lips. "You already have my attention, woman." Jake kissed her with the sound of the sea rushing and hurling around them. Sea water pooled at their feet, but she didn't feel cold. Not one bit.

When they broke, she was breathless, her mind a swirling vortex of emotion that she couldn't quite catch or tame. She wanted to freeze in this space, to forget about going back to her to-do list and worries over the future.

He stepped back, his eyes amused and full of light. How could she worry while looking into eyes like those?

Jake squeezed her hand and brought it to his lips. "C'mon. Let's go back to the house so I can call my sisters and let them all yell at me."

Back at the house, they dropped their sandy flip-flops on the front porch and stumbled inside, laughing as they did. The Holloway house always seemed so lively when she was a kid. She never minded being an only child, not really, but on occasion, when she'd look over and see the glow from the house's lights and all the people moving around inside, she would wonder what it might have been like to live there.

The kitchen was nearly done, yet not one hundred percent usable quite yet. She padded over to the fridge, feeling comfortable enough to poke around inside. "Want a steak salad?"

Jake tossed his keys into a metal dish. "You mean leftover steak and a salad? Hm. Not sure if there's enough for that— but you can go ahead and eat what's left."

She pulled the leftover steak, lettuce, and various vegetables out of the fridge. "Trust me. I can toss this all together into the best salad you've ever tasted." She grabbed olive oil, red wine vinegar, salt, and pepper from the small table where Jake had stashed the items during the remodel.

"Hopefully I'll find some time to put everything away. Or maybe I'll leave it all for Maggie to do when it's her turn at the house."

She waved a hand in the air. "I got it. No problem." She tried not to think about how soon that transition he mentioned might take place. What would happen when he went back to LA? When he was no longer just across the small, sandy divide between their two houses?

Jake stepped up to Daisy from behind and nuzzled her neck. "I'm enjoying this ..."

"Shoo. I'm trying to make your dinner."

He laughed and let her go. "Don't bother the woman while she's cooking. I hear you loud and clear." Jake's laughter continued as he walked across the room and switched on his laptop.

She glanced at the clock, hoping there'd be enough time

to feed them both before the weekly call started. From what she'd heard, things could get rather rowdy when the five siblings were all together, talking at once.

Again, something she, as an only child, personally knew nothing about.

Minutes later, Daisy curled her legs beneath herself on the couch while Jake propped his feet on the coffee table. Both held bowls of steak salad marinated with oil, vinegar, and seasonings.

"This is excellent," he said, digging into his salad. "You weren't kidding about this being the best salad ever. I'm impressed."

"My mom was a whiz, well, she is a whiz at throwing leftovers together in creative ways. This is one of my favorites."

He nodded, but didn't say anything more. She noticed again that subtle change in him whenever she mentioned her mother. She was beginning to wonder if he was as worried over their future as she was.

Jake wolfed down the rest of his dinner and darted for the computer, the familiar ring of his phone alerting him that it was time. "Just stay where you are," he said when she began to get up. "You're fine. *Mangia!*"

She laughed when he used the Italian term for *eat!* that his parents did whenever she was invited to come over for pizza or spaghetti or whatever they were having on a lazy Sunday afternoon.

Maggie was the first to show up on the call, which from what she remembered about the oldest sister, was not surprising. "Hi, Jake."

"Mags."

"Is that Daisy over there on the couch? Hey, Daisy!"

"Hi! Hope you don't mind me. Just finishing up dinner."

"Which she made," Jake cut in. "And it was excellent, by the way."

Maggie laughed. "Glad you two are getting along okay out there."

Jake sent Daisy a wink that sent a sweet chill right through her.

"Hello, children." Lacy appeared, goblet in hand, smirk on her face.

Grace was up next, looking harried. "Sorry I'm late. Brutal day. Big case in the office that I'm helping Chase on."

Maggie frowned. "Even on a Sunday? Did you miss church?"

"Have to be in court very early tomorrow, so yes, even on Sunday. And no, we went to church."

"That stinks," Lacy said. "Not the going to church part, of course."

Bella's angelic face appeared in the fourth box. The entire production played out like the opening of The Brady Bunch. "What stinks?" Bella asked.

"Grace-y poo and her man had to work all day today," Lacy drawled.

Jake clapped his hands together. "Okay, how about we get on with this."

Even from across the room, Daisy noticed how Maggie peered into the screen, her ample bosom filling it up. "How's the kitchen coming along, Jake?" Maggie asked. "Have you made any progress?"

"Funny you should ask." He picked up his laptop, walked over to the kitchen, and turned it around for all to see. From her perch on the couch, Daisy could hear the gasps.

"It's so beautiful," Bella said. "I wish our momma could have seen that."

Lacy answered. "She would have thought it too pretty to cook in."

"Good job," Grace said, glasses on her nose, her attention elsewhere. Her shoulders bounced as if she were typing.

"Wait a second. Hold on." Maggie's voice cut through the chatter. "Tell me you didn't put a Viking stove in there. And I will literally kill you if that refrigerator has Dutch doors— those are the most expensive on the market." She fanned herself, her face turning red. "Please tell me it's not a Bosch."

"It's not a Bosch," Jake said.

She leaned into the screen again. "Liar! Oh Jake, what were you thinking spending money like that?"

Jake slid a glance at Daisy. She met his gaze, shrugged, and re-focused her attention on what was left of her dinner.

"Don't worry about it, Maggie. I've got it covered."

"How?"

"One of my connections gave me a sweet deal. Put it out of your mind, all right?"

Grace stopped typing and suddenly looked up. "Speaking of things on my mind, Chase and I are concerned about you, Jake." She glanced at her sisters. "I figured now was as good a time as any to bring this up."

The proverbial pin was dropping. Daisy could feel it. She glanced at Jake, who seemed agitated, his gaze darting toward the door. Was he looking for a way to escape?

Lacy swirled her wine in her glass. "What's got you in such a snit, Grace? You're usually one of the calmer ones." She gulped her wine and threw a pointed look toward Maggie.

Grace started typing again, her eyes tracking side to side as if looking something up that she found online. "Hold on a sec. Okay ... here it is. An article." She looked up. "What's this about you being in trouble with the coastal commission?"

Jake slid that guarded look at her again. "My lawyer's on it, Grace. Nothing to worry about."

"Really? You know you could talk to Chase about it, if you don't think I have enough experience yet." After Grace and Chase saved her mother's life, Daisy learned that they were lawyers. Grace only recently passed the bar, but her husband was a seasoned attorney.

"I appreciate that," Jake said, his voice steady and lower than usual. She guessed he had switched on his corporate voice for his sisters. "Now if we could get back to the matters pertaining to this house and how we're going to deal with the rest of our parents' wishes ..."

Lacy spoke up. "Maggie's taking my place next month."

Grace said, "You're kidding. You okay with this, Mags?"

Daisy took a surreptitious glance at the screen. Even from here she could see the graying circles under Maggie's eyes. An effect from her lack of money? She and Jake had not talked anymore about Maggie's situation, but from what she gathered, things were tough for her right now. She glanced at Jake, noting the fretful look on his face. He was staring at his phone, caught up in some other drama.

After a few seconds, Maggie sat forward again, nodding at Grace, a smile burgeoning. "I'm good. Greg's been chipping in finally, so that's been helpful."

"About time," Lacy said about Maggie's ex. "Hope you're not thinking about taking him back, though."

Maggie waved away Lacy's concerns, but the smile lingered on her face. "No worries. Anyway, I had to make a few adjustments in my work schedule"—she paused, as if choosing her words carefully—"but it's going to work out fine, especially since Eva will be on summer break."

Jake nodded once as if he'd heard the last few minutes of conversation. "Good—"

Grace cut in. "It's important that we all make sure to let our executor know when we've completed our month at the house."

"Got it," Jake said. "I still have some time here"—he slid a glance at Daisy before returning his attention to his sisters—"but I'll check in with him at the end of my shift, so to speak."

Daisy didn't hear much else for the rest of the call. All she could think about was that Jake would be leaving soon—and they had only just begun.

9

His sisters exhausted him. Jake had felt this for some time, but until tonight's call, he'd never clearly identified that truth. He yawned and looked over his notes. Somehow in the last hour, he had promised to update the first floor bath so that Maggie would have some luxury to come home to.

He glanced over at the empty couch, an unavoidable sinking in his stomach. Daisy had stepped out of the room at some point during the call. Maybe it hadn't been such a grand idea to have her here, listening to his sisters' squabbles. More than that, what had she been thinking about the reality that his time in Colibri was almost up? Of course, she had always known this was a temporary stay, that he had work—and legal troubles—to deal with back in Los Angeles.

He sighed and leaned forward, his temple against his hand.

"Tired?"

Jake looked up to find Daisy emerging from the hall

wearing oversized light-pink sweats, her feet bare, her blonde locks piled into a bun, tendrils framing her face. Absolutely irresistible.

She smiled shyly at him. "You okay?" She sat down beside him, and he grasped her hand, intertwining his fingers with hers.

He quirked a grin at her. "I'm feeling revitalized all of a sudden."

"Yeah?" Daisy kissed him on the nose, and when he took in the expression on her face, he noticed a certain sadness in her eyes. He wanted to ignore it. *Mañana, mañana* ... but that felt terribly unfair.

"Aw, Daisy," he whispered. "I'm sure you're wondering what's been happening with my business. Grace made it sound pretty bad, didn't she?"

"You don't have to tell me if you're not ready."

He shook his head. "It's not that I don't want to tell you— I just hate talking about it."

She quirked a sad smile at him. "I gathered that."

He let out a groan then snapped an unguarded look at her. "The company I own is being threatened with an enormous fine—a record dollar amount—by the coastal commission for a bait-and-switch building project that I knew nothing about."

Daisy gasped. "Oh no. Do you think there's a traitor in your company?"

Jake shook his head. "I wish it were that simple. I headed up this project myself from the start. The lead contractor, who is also in hot water with the commission, has been blaming my firm for this, but he's wrong."

He sighed and continued. "It's all on me, Daisy. I made a

mistake by working with that contractor. He said all the right things to get the contract, threw around the best numbers, but in the end, it wasn't worth it."

"Do you think he's the one who set you up?"

"I know it." Jake released another sigh. It felt good to share his no-good, horrible news with someone other than his legal team. Despite how enormous the problem had become, somehow Jake felt more at ease having Daisy beside him. "Yes, I know that he had something to do with it, though I can't prove it—yet."

"Oh, Jake. I'm so sorry. What does your attorney say?"

He leaned back. "He's been trying, without success, to depose the foreman on the project. A guy by the name of Billy Bask. We think he altered my plans after they were signed off on, making it appear that they had been approved. My guess is that they're paying Billy to hide." He glowered. "Who suddenly turns invisible in this century with social media showing people's every move?"

"Has your lawyer hired an investigator?"

Jake nodded. "Absolutely." He lifted his phone and scrolled through his email, stopping on one. "The guy he hired thinks he's getting closer. It's all very cloak and dagger right now. I just want Billy found and the truth dragged out of him."

Daisy exhaled, the sound of it like chimes in a stiff wind. He needed that right now more than anything. Her touch, her soothing voice prodding him along on their daily talks. He glanced down at her, his gaze brushing over her eyes and that spattering of freckles across her nose, before landing on her soft lips. With his business hanging precariously, not to mention his impending move back to the City, how long could this last?

DAISY SNUGGLED UP NEXT to Jake on the couch and tucked her legs beneath her. As he told her about his legal troubles, the gravity of the situation weighed on her. Despite her lack of knowledge in the matter, she could at least lend a sympathetic ear and provide comfort. Unfortunately, that's all she could do.

She glanced up at him, noticing the way his gaze slid to hers, making her pulse race. He bent down slightly until his lips touched hers with a soft and gentle kiss. Soon, his hand found the back of her head and cradled her there as he took the kiss deeper. Daisy reached up and touched his jawline, wanting more of him, but knowing they were moving down dangerous waters. She couldn't think, couldn't reason any longer, her desire for him drawing her further into the abyss she had once dreamed about.

Her phone rang and Daisy jumped.

Jake groaned.

She glanced at the screen and frowned. "It's ... it's the rehab facility. I-I have to take this."

"Of course." Jake sat up and gestured for her to take the call.

"Hello?" Daisy stood up, phone in her ear, suddenly feeling the need to pace.

"Good news, Daisy," Lynette said. "Your mother's paperwork is all ready. I suspect the doctor will sign these discharge papers tomorrow morning, though it will be some time before she can go home."

"Okay, so he'll be looking over everything tomorrow," she repeated.

"Right. But like I said, sometimes it takes some time to get everything together. I just wanted to give you a heads-up that we're getting closer."

Daisy exhaled, relief flooding her. She would still had time left to work on her mother's house, to figure out her aftercare, to get the electricity back on ...

Lynette cut back in. "She will probably be ready to go home with you by early afternoon."

"Early afternoon ... when?"

Lynette chuckled. "Why, tomorrow, of course."

Daisy stared into the living room, seeing nothing, her mind trying to wrap itself around her sudden reality. This should have been a moment of joy, but ... she wasn't ready. Guilt needled her that it wasn't exactly euphoria she was feeling at the moment. Suddenly her to-do list had grown at the same rate that her available time had shrunk.

Daisy thanked Lynette for the call and assured her she would arrive on time at the facility tomorrow afternoon to pick up her mother. She hung up and slid a look at Jake who had moved into the kitchen where he appeared to be idly fiddling with a faucet handle.

"I'm sure you heard ... my mother's about ready to come home."

He turned and braced himself against the sink, a cloud working over his expression. "Are you ready for her?"

Daisy sighed and shook her head. "Not really. So much to do, you know?"

He pressed his lips together and nodded, though something about the way he did it made her wonder what was going on in that handsome head of his. He looked distant, all of a sudden—a far cry from where they had been moments before. Maybe she should be grateful.

She approached him, reached up, and touched his face. "I appreciate you letting me stay here, Jake. It's made my life so much easier." And so much more complicated, too.

His gaze slid down to her as she lifted a hand to stroke his face with her hand. He covered her hand with his. "I'd do it again. In a heartbeat."

Though his words were sweet, Jake's tone sounded tinged with relief, as if he, too, had enjoyed their time together, but was fully ready for her to move on. Or was she being too dramatic? Daisy pasted on a smile and took a step back. "Guess I'll go to bed now. Have a lot to do in the morning, you know?"

He nodded. "I know."

She kissed him on the cheek. "'Night, Jake."

He didn't move, but simply stared after her. "Good night."

Daisy headed down the hall to the cute bedroom with the big old whale comforter on it, feeling anything but comforted.

10

After a whirlwind of a morning, the electric company finally arrived the next afternoon to restore power. Daisy wasted no time restocking the fridge with an abundance of fresh fruits and vegetables. She also removed all tarps, tape, and other signs of her painting marathon. Despite the chaos, Daisy had managed to work miracles in just one small portion of a day.

Jake had popped in once to check up on her, and although she appreciated his help moving a few pieces of furniture around so her mother could use the downstairs bedroom, she had also sensed some distance growing between them. Fortunately, she'd been much too busy to think too much about that or what the near future would look like for them.

By late afternoon, her mother was home.

"It's so beautiful in here, Daisy!"

Her mother had said the same thing about twelve times since she'd arrived. She was laying on the couch with a fluffy throw over her legs, admiring the living room as if a designer had come through and replaced everything.

"You know these are all your things in here, Momma, right?" Daisy pointed to the arrangement of still-life flower paintings on the wall. "Those were spread all over the house. I just decided to put them together so they could catch the natural light in here."

"You have done a mar ... a marvel ... oh."

Daisy handed her mother a glass of water. "I think you mean marvelous, right?"

Wren gave Daisy a sad smile. "I am still having trouble saying some words."

"Don't worry about that at all. Remember what your nurse said? You have come a long way, but some things will take a little more time." Daisy slapped her hands on her lap. "If you're comfortable here, I think I'll get dinner started. Are you hungry?"

"I am, dear. Thank you."

Daisy peeked out the window on her way to the kitchen. Twilight was setting in, yet not one light shone in Jake's house. He hadn't mentioned to her that he was going anywhere. Not that it was any of her business, really. Still, she wondered if he had plans to pop in later and see her mother. Or her. Earlier when he had been here, he hadn't mentioned coming by again, but she held out hope that he would.

In the kitchen, she glanced at the list of foods recommended for her mother by the rehab center, most of them bland and filled with starch and empty calories. Gross. She set the list aside and instead began making a simple stir fry with vegetables and chicken, along with a pot of brown rice.

Cooking had a way of awakening the senses to all the good things in life. But the solitary nature of it also opened up the mind to think, and unfortunately, Daisy found herself dwelling on the way Jake seemed to retreat from her last night. One minute he was telling her his secrets as they clung to each other. And the next, he's puttering around the kitchen and acting like they were simply ... friends.

Her breath caught in her throat. Had she read too much into their relationship? Accepted his interest as an answer to her teenaged prayer that he would notice her? Jake had said he was falling for her, but today he seemed rather emotionless. Daisy shut her eyes. Had she been wrong to trust him?

Her mother's voice pulled her from her desperate thoughts. "Daisy? Smells like something is burning."

She gasped and shot a look at the pot of rice. All the water had been absorbed. Daisy grabbed a hot pad and moved the pot to a cool burner. "Thanks, Mom! I'll be right out."

Daisy gave her head a tight shake. She had too much on her mind to obsess over Jake's sudden shift in attitude. Quickly, she dished up bowls of stir fry and brown rice and brought them out to the coffee table. "Small bites, momma, okay?"

Her mother's eyes glistened. "You take such good care of me."

"Because I love you."

Wren finished a bit of food. "Have you seen Jake lately?"

Daisy stilled. How much should she tell her mother about her relationship with Jake? She neither cared to get her mother's hopes up nor cause them to plummet, as hers were on the brink of doing. "I saw him earlier today, as a matter of fact. He came in to help me rearrange the furniture in your bedroom."

"Oh, how sweet of him! You know, he was a rascal as a child, but I've always known his heart to be kind. And he's smart, too."

Daisy smiled. "I didn't realize you knew him all that well."

"Oh, he would come through sometimes when I'd be over there visiting. His parents both spoke so well of him that I feel as if I know him, too." Her mother took another bite of dinner, her face contemplative. "Do you think you could ask him to come over soon? I have something for him."

Daisy tilted her head. "Like a gift?"

Her mother nodded. "Yes. I would really like to see him. Will you ask him to come see me?"

"Sure. If I see him around tomorrow, I'll stop by and ask him to come." She tried to sound nonchalant, when really, her head was full of questions.

"That would be lovely."

When her mother had eaten all she could, Daisy cleared the dishes and dumped them into a sink full of soapy water. She spent the next hour helping her get ready for bed by washing up and taking her medicines. Soon, her mother drifted off to sleep, content to be back in her own home.

Daisy wandered back into the living room, her body spent, but her mind still strangely active. She stole a glance out the window, noticing the blaze of lights at the Holloway home, yet Jake had not called her. Myriad thoughts began to pummel her mind, such as what would happen when Jake's month at the beach house was over? How could he afford to help Maggie the way he did? And why, if he was in trouble, hadn't he bothered to ask his lawyer of a sister or her husband to help him?

After a moment more of staring into the night, Daisy turned away from the window, more thoughts rumbling through her brain. Why did Jake close up every time her mother's name came up in conversation? And how would he respond when Daisy told him that her mother had something to give him?

Daisy took a second glance at her phone its screen annoyingly blank. Then she retreated down the hall to climb into bed and think.

JAKE STOOD on a bank of sand that jutted out over the ocean. The sea had pummeled the shore last night, creating cliffs where there had been none before. He had intended to run along the water's edge, but found it swallowed up by rogue waves and occasional drop-offs filled with seawater.

He sighed, his breath floating away on a stiff breeze. Last night, when Daisy said she would be leaving soon, all he had wanted to do was pull her into his embrace and hold her there. But he had let the moment pass him by, obliterated by confusion. He missed the feel of her, the touch of her fingers on his jaw, the taste of her kiss, chaste as they were. His thoughts of her seduced him into thinking, though, that he could forget the things that haunted him, that pulled him away from fully enjoying a relationship with her.

He had no idea what he could do about that.

With the sand unwilling to provide him a flat place to run, he instead walked forcefully, his feet plowing a path through deep powder. Jake had awoken this morning to several texts that had set his mind further on edge. His lawyer texted that, though they had not definitively located Billy, they *had* uncovered some information that could very well smoke him out of wherever he was hiding. Jake had immediately placed a call to Mike, but had to leave a message. His shoulders tensed. Paid the guy a lot of money for his calls to be going to voicemail ...

It was the text from Maggie, though, that had him on alert the most: *Good news, I think. My ex is coming around. May be a reunion soon. Wish me luck!*

Jake re-read the text, frowning. His oldest sister was the most organized, centered, and reliable woman he knew. But when it came to her heart, her judgment failed her. He wanted to text her back with one word: Run! But though he believed that to be the sagest advice he could give her, Jake did not want to hurt Maggie. He tucked his phone into his back pocket, determined to let the churn of the sea clear his mind before he faced the rest of his day.

By the time Jake arrived at the house, he felt revived and ready. He left his trainers on the porch and swung the door open. Daisy stood in the living room wearing yoga pants and a hoodie, her arms hugging her middle. Her eyes zeroed in on his. "Hey," she said.

He closed the door behind him. "Hi. Everything all right?" He approached her, but she didn't move, just stared up at him. "Daisy?"

She rubbed her lips together. "You haven't been by."

He sensed the question in her remark. "I've been ... there's been a lot of development ..." He blew out a breath and tried to reach out to her. "Sorry. My mind's been overrun lately."

Daisy's brows dipped. She watched him as if questioning the honesty of his response. "Okay."

He fiddled with her hair. "Things okay with you?"

"You mean with my mother."

"Yeah. With ... with your mother. Are things settling down for you?"

She quirked her head and unfolded her arms from her body. "What are you doing, Jake?"

"I don't understand."

"You know, I thought your sudden freeze out might have something to do with the fact that you'll be leaving here soon. I mean, we haven't exactly talked about that, but you seemed to get antsy the other night, so I figured you were thinking about it."

He reached out to her. "Daisy ..."

She shook her head. "But the more I thought about it, the more I realized something: Every time my mother's name comes up, you get this cold look in your eye. It's like you, I don't know, don't like her or something." She paused, searching his face. "Do you have something against my mother, Jake?"

He eyed her, slayed by the look of distrust in her face. It knifed him in the gut. But telling Daisy how he felt would mean exposing something less-than-complimentary about her mother. Maggie had warned him, but he hadn't listened. Now he had no way to escape, except to lie.

Jake pulled her into a hug, despite her stilted response. "I'm sorry, Daisy. I've just been so preoccupied with everything. I didn't mean to make you or your mother feel unimportant."

Daisy looked up at him, warily. "She wants to see you. Will you come today?"

His mind scurried for an answer. "Hm. Not today, but soon."

She took a step back and pointed at him. "There. That face you're giving me." She wagged her head, her eyes narrowed. "You're being evasive. Wish I knew why."

Jake pressed his tongue to the inside of his cheek. He needed to confront this, but not now. Deflect, deflect. "Now you're imagining things."

She broke away from him. "Please." Daisy crossed her arms. "Are you wealthy, Jake? Like ... really wealthy?"

He sputtered. "Does it matter?"

"You mean, would I like you more? No."

"That's not what I meant. It's just ..." He raked a hand through his hair. He was falling hard for her and didn't give a rat's behind if she knew the balance in his bank account. But it changed things. Money *always* changed things. His father had warned him about that when he was a kid. That's why his father made him read *The Millionaire Next Door* and other books like it. So he wouldn't get caught up in image or impressing people. He'd learned this the hard way about the women who came after him once they sensed his wealth.

Admittedly, he had not once thought of any of those women the way he thought about Daisy—as *the one*. That realization startled him. He swallowed, his pride bearing down on him. She deserved more. He knew that. But did he have it to give her?

Daisy stepped quickly across the room, opened the front

door, and stopped. She turned a look over her shoulder. "It was fun while it lasted, Jake."

"Daisy, don't."

"My mother has a gift for you, but it's up to you whether you care to retrieve it." She sighed. "You know where to find us." On the way out, she shut the door hard and through the side window, he watched her jog back to her mother's home without another look his way.

11

D aisy showed her mother's home health nurse around the house before stepping outside for a much-needed run on the beach. She half-wished the morning had dawned gray, as so many beach days did on the central coast. The lack of color would further feed her empty heart and assist in the wallowing she had been doing over the past twenty-four hours.

Jake had not shown up.

He texted once, apologizing. Duty called and all that— something about installing countertops. She had shrugged off his message, unwilling to let him back into the deepest places of her mind and soul.

The tide was out, and as she took to the sand, which seemed to stretch for miles, she shucked her hoodie off and tied it around her waist. She started off fast, but slowed her pace once, realizing the fuel of discontent behind her speed. A sea lion broke the surface of the water, the curiosity in its shiny face lightening her mood some, forcing her to reflect.

Her life was good. Her mother had survived a difficult situation and health issue. She loved her work. Had a little bit of money in the bank to fall back on, if she needed it. And she had discovered the joy and self-sufficiency of running. A grin found her. Short people didn't run. Her high school counselor had given her that bit of unwelcome advice when she was searching for a sport. Until senior year, she had believed it—that's when she noticed Haley Ross's thigh gap and realized that Haley was no taller than her. Daisy started running that afternoon. *Take that, haters.*

Daisy's phone buzzed in her pocket, but she dared not look at it. The stress of the past couple of days was starting to leave her and she didn't want anything to mess that up. In front of her, two children, a boy and a girl, worked on a sandcastle. The girl's hands and legs were caked with wet sand. Her tongue was sticking out of her mouth, caught between her teeth as she worked furiously on the tall and unwieldy structure before the tide would come in and pull it out to sea. The boy's limbs were equally coated in sand as he hauled a bucket full of water from the shore. Daisy slowed as she passed them, watching the boy dump the water into a long and winding moat.

If only relationships could be as simple as building a sandcastle at the beach. Then again, as she reminded Jake, they couldn't even agree on proper sandcastle building when they were kids.

Daisy picked up her pace, once again stuffing away thoughts of her battered heart. Maybe the time apart from Jake was for the best. Her face heated thinking of how quickly their passion had ignited. If her mother's nurse hadn't called the other night, Daisy could very well have fallen into a place with Jake that would be much harder to disengage from, let alone forget.

She shook her head. The past month was not real life. Though it might not look like it from all the work being done on the Holloway home, Jake had been on vacation. He had been away from the stress of his work—and the pending fines and litigation—and lolling on the beach in between sprucing up the kitchen and now the downstairs bath. How could she have expected him to make something permanent out of a temporary situation? Not that she was giving him a pass. Daisy was choosing to be a realist and to see things the way they really were. It was the only way to protect herself.

A tear rolled out of her eye, surprising her. She wicked it away with a swipe of her hand. She knew better than this. He'd broken her heart when they were kids, and now that she had let her guard down, he was on his way to breaking it again. Only this time, it would be much harder to put back together.

Daisy picked up the pace determined not to let that happen again. She wouldn't.

"Why hasn't Jake come to see me? Did you tell him I have a gift for him?"

Daisy turned away from her mother before answering. Otherwise, her mom might have seen something in Daisy's face that she didn't care to share. "I've told him, Momma. Be patient. He is remodeling their kitchen and bathroom and also doing some work for his business from home." She paused, not sure if she should be making promises when it came to Jake. "I'm sure he will stop by when he can."

Her mother leaned toward the window. "He's so tall."

"Hmm?"

"There," she said, pointing out the window. "Oh good. It looks like he's coming over here right now."

Hesitantly, Daisy peered out the window to see Jake stalking across the sand toward her front porch. Reflexively, she smoothed her hair with a hand and licked her lips, which she had left makeup-free today.

"Answer the door," her mother said.

She frowned. He hadn't even knocked and no way would she let him think her overanxious about seeing him. She would not explain that to her mother either. Would open her up to too many questions ...

"Hurry!" her mother said.

Daisy sighed. She opened the door to find Jake standing on the stoop, fist raised as if readying himself to knock.

"Hello," he said.

"Jake."

He raised a brow. "Can I come in?"

Silently, she stepped back to let him enter.

Her mother squealed, obviously unaware of the standoff. "Jake Holloway! Come here and let me look at you."

"Hello, Mrs. Mcafee."

"Oh stop that. I'm Wren, but you know that already."

"How are you feeling?"

Wren wiggled in her spot on the couch, pulling herself out of a slouching position. She laid her folded hands in her lap. "I am feeling much better. Oh Jake. I will forever be in debt to your sister Grace and that handsome husband of hers—what is his name again?"

"It's Chase," Jake said.

Wren laughed and clapped her hands. "That's right. Their names rhyme. I had forgotten that."

After the laughter died away, an uncomfortable silence fell over the room. Daisy still stood awkwardly near Jake. "Momma, you said something about a gift you had? For Jake?"

"That's right. Where did I leave it? Let me think." Her mother frowned, a deep wedge forming between her eyes. "Daisy, would you go upstairs and look in my bureau? I think you'll find it there. It's a frame, wrapped in butcher paper."

Daisy hurried upstairs, her mind a blur. She wanted to sink into her bed, to hide away from the tension hovering like an invisible vapor in her mother's living room. What was she looking for again?

Her mother's voice trilled from downstairs. "Did you find it?"

Right. The wrapped frame. She opened her mother's bottom drawer and felt around for something beneath all the miscellaneous fabric tucked away in there. Scarves, mismatched socks, doilies and woven fabrics without a purpose ... there. Her fingers bumped up against something. A wrapped item shaped like a frame. Just like her mother said.

She descended the stairs and took a seat on the couch beside her mother, holding up the package. "Is this what you meant?"

The old woman's face beamed. She nodded and took the

package from her hands, then held it out for Jake. "This is for you."

He cast a questioning look at Daisy, but all she could do was turn up her palms and shrug. Slowly, Jake tore away the paper. His mouth fell open and his eyes darkened by a dip of his brows. He looked up. "Where ... where did you get this?"

"Your father gave it to me. Well, he asked me to frame it for you. He was so proud of you, Jake. Sadly, he died before I was able to have it done."

Daisy stretched forward. "What is it?"

Jake lifted his chin, his expression stricken. "It's the first plan I created when I was learning CAD."

"CAD? As in ...?"

"Computer-aided drafting, yes. You probably know it as a program for architects and designers." He turned to Wren, his expression pained, his voice uncharacteristically hushed. "What else were you doing for my father?"

"What do you mean, son?"

Jake held the framed drawing in one hand, as his other hand scraped through his head of dark hair. He pivoted, no shred of a smile on his face.

Slowly, Daisy stood, one hand touching her mother's shoulder lightly. "Jake? What's going on?"

He turned his gaze on her, his jaw set. He dropped his gaze toward her mother. "Maybe Wren should answer that question, once and for all."

Wren frowned. "I'm confused, dear."

Jake darted a glance at Wren and sighed. "My mother was very sick during the past couple of years of her life. I'm not proud of the fact that my siblings and I weren't around the way we should have been back then."

Wren nodded, her eyes dewy, downcast at the mention of Jake's mother. Daisy knew how close they were, that they were great friends who shared a love of pie, lavender, and swapping stories about their children.

He inhaled sharply as if gathering strength, then Jake zeroed in on her mother. "But I have to ask you this question, Wren. Were you ... and my father ... having an affair?"

Daisy gasped. "Jake!"

He swiveled his gaze to Daisy, his eyes pleading, but all she could do was shake her head at him. How dare he?

Wren elicited a high-pitched sigh. "No, dear. Absolutely not." She cupped both of her hands over her mouth, as if in a prayer position.

Daisy moved in front of her mother, shielding her. "Get out of here, Jake."

He reached for her, but she turned away from him. "I'm sorry. But I have to know," he whispered, holding up the framed picture. "And from this, I think I do."

Wren attempted to push Daisy aside. "Stop it! The both of you, stop it right now."

Daisy hugged her body and sat close to her mother. "Why didn't you say anything about this to me the past few weeks, Jake? Why wait until my poor mother is home recovering to unload your accusation?"

Pain crossed his features. "I didn't want to hurt you."

"Too late," she spat. She fought off the tears that flooded her sinuses and pooled around her eyes.

"Oh dear, oh dear." Wren rubbed her daughter's back. "Don't cry, honey. Jake, sit down."

Jake hesitated but lowered himself into a chair and leaned forward, his elbows digging into his thighs. "I'm sorry the way this has come about, Wren. But I saw you and my father once. Remember?"

Wren scrunched her face, her lips pursed. Daisy glanced back at her, unsure of who to believe. Maybe her mother was too sick to remember what had happened so long ago. Then again, except for occasional forgetfulness and lack of energy, she was pretty much the same mom Daisy had left to travel the world.

"I'm sorry, but no," Wren said. "I don't know why you would have thought such a terrible thing about your father."

Daisy cut in. "And about you, too, Mom!"

Jake spoke softly now. "I had come home to check on my mother. She was, well, less than healthy." He shook his head. "I had no idea that her mind had deteriorated to such an extent. I stayed the night, but awoke in the middle of it, unable to sleep. And so I came out to the deck—"

Wren gasped. "And you saw us."

Daisy swiveled sharply. "Mom? Wait. Is this true?"

Wren shook her head. "We were only smoking!"

Jake frowned. "What?"

"Your father liked to smoke cigars, as did I, but your mother hated the smell of them. Always said she wouldn't kiss him if he smoked them. So he didn't. Until … well, until she didn't notice anymore." Wren sighed, a slightly guilty smile on her face. "I had ordered a big box of Cubans and your father would come over and smoke them with me about once per week. Honey, it was purely innocent."

Jake leaned his forehead into his palm, clearly shocked by this news. If Daisy weren't so angry with him, she might have found this hilarious. But right now, she wanted to wring his neck for jumping to conclusions. Of all the stupid ideas to obsess over. All this time he thought that her father and his mother had been lovers? No wonder he had made himself invisible once her mother had come home!

"I don't know what to say." Jake's head hung, but he was peering up at her, noticeably humbled. Daisy almost felt sorry for him ... almost.

"There's more, dear," Wren said. She reached out to her daughter as if preparing her for what she was about to say. "Jake, your father was a very generous man. And he, well, he was helping me. Financially."

Daisy shot up. "What?"

"Don't be angry with him, Daisy. Please. I couldn't bear it."

"But Daddy left me a trust fund. How could he do that, if you were—"

"Broke?"

Daisy put a hand to her chest as if her airways had narrowed. She could barely breathe.

Wren continued. "Your father and I set up that trust fund for you when you were little. It was written so that you could have it by your twenty-first birthday, no matter where he and I were. It just happened that he died before then."

"But why are you so broke?"

Her mother sighed. "We made an investment with great hope, but unfortunately, it didn't take off like we thought and we lost most of our savings." She turned to Jake, her voice breaking. "Your father knew about it, and he made sure I was taken care of. He was a good man."

The room fell silent as if all three of them had become caught up in their own private thoughts. Jake was the first to break the silence.

"I'm so sorry for what I accused you of, Wren." He paused. "Can you forgive me?"

Wren smiled. "Of course, I can. Life is too short to hold grudges." She patted his knee. "I've learned that."

Jake reached for her hand. "Thank you." He let her hand go and held up the framed picture of his drawing. "And thank you for this. You'll never know how much it means to me."

"You're very welcome."

Jake turned to Daisy. "Talk to me?"

She hesitated, but ultimately followed him outside, anger boiling beneath the surface. They didn't go to his house, but out onto the sand, beneath the dark expanse of sky. The ocean's tumult provided an appropriate backdrop for Daisy's mood and she spun on him. "What was I to you, Jake? Just some distraction?"

"No. You were a surprise to me, Daisy."

"Why? Because on the way to vilifying my mother, you thought you'd play games with her daughter's heart and it worked?"

He shook his head, imploring her with an unwavering gaze. "I'm not that guy."

She pointed up at him, barely able to keep the shake out of her voice. "You're exactly that guy. I thought I'd learned my lesson with you, but I guess I'm not that smart. You haven't changed a bit."

Jake stared at her, unmoving, that framed picture still under his arm. "We're not kids anymore."

"Then why do you keep secrets like a teenager? You could have told me what you thought about our parents."

"Your mother kept a secret too."

"Don't blame my mother." Even to her own ears she sounded weary, sad. "I wish I had known how difficult it was for her. I wouldn't have been traveling the world all this time had I known."

"And that's exactly why she never told you. I admire her."

She landed a gaze on him. "What about your secret gifts to Maggie? Has this taught you anything at all about the danger of keeping some things buried?"

"I'm not ready to change my stance on that."

"Even though your sister thinks her ex has been sending her money?"

Jake recoiled. "What? How do you know that?"

Daisy stared at him, open-mouthed. What had he missed? "She pretty much said so on the call the other night. I guess you weren't listening."

Jake's shoulders clenched visibly. He puffed out his cheeks and blew out a long, slow breath, then leveled a gaze at her. "Maybe you're right about me, Daisy. Because, contrary to what you think, you are very smart. But me?" He shook his head, a sad tilt to his mouth. "I've still got a lot to learn."

They stared at each other, waves crashing behind them, the sound neither soothing nor welcome. Daisy barely heard Jake as he bent forward and whispered, "Goodbye, Daisy," turned on his heels, and left.

12

J ake climbed upstairs to the master bedroom he'd hardly looked at since arriving in Colibri Beach. He tossed his shirt across the room and laid on his parents' old queen-sized bed. How had he gotten so many important things wrong? Wren? His father? Maggie? What Daisy said about his sister's situation gripped him. Had he really missed her saying something so crucial? The last thing he wanted to do was drive Maggie back to that jockstrap.

He flipped over onto his back, cradling his head with his hands and looking squarely above him at the sloped knotty pine ceiling. So many shapes and pictures in an old ceiling like this. He remembered the times he would sprawl out here on hot nights, grateful for the single air conditioning unit his parents kept in the window.

If only this ceiling, with its swirls and figures, could give him answers to the questions burning inside of him. Like, why hadn't he been able to see, until now, where the anger he had been carrying had come from? Jake closed his eyes, remembering his parents, how they loved each other—and teased each other fiercely. He missed them, even though he and his father often landed on the wrong side of each other.

In the end, Jake realized, he had been angry with his father for something that was never really his fault. The night that Jake had come home for a surprise visit, he hadn't been prepared. His mother wasn't herself. She had eaten dinner with the two of them in near silence. Wasn't like her —at all. Throughout the evening, his father had smiled at her, patted her hand, and ushered her to bed.

And Jake had gone to bed angry for not knowing, until then, the extent of her illness. Later, when he had spotted his dad with Wren out there on that balcony, he became incensed. Had made his own conclusions and directed his anger there.

Wren—and his father—had become his scapegoats.

Jake sat up and picked up the framed design Wren had saved for him. He had forgotten all about the first effort at doing what he now loves. The drawing of a home much like his family's beach house was riddled with errors. He knew just by glancing at the design behind glass that the structure could never be built as he had laid it out. Didn't matter, though. His father had chosen to keep it, long after Jake had virtually thrown it away.

He smiled at it, ruefully. Maybe it was time to get back to the basics and do what he loved so much—build houses. Old styles, like this one. Places with wide-open rooms where families and friends gathered, built with warm weathered beams and interesting nooks.

A picture popped into his mind. Not a house ... but a

church. An oversized chapel, really, with lines like an old beach house. He might not have noticed the state of Colibri Church if Daisy hadn't mentioned it ... hadn't taken photos of the old place. A twist of something turned in his gut— guilt, perhaps? He shoved it aside, the gabled structure blazing into his mind.

The idea of giving new life to something that had seen better days satisfied some sort of lost part of his artistic soul and he knew he would pursue it. Maybe even find the happiness that had been missing from his life.

Happiness ... missing from his life.

Daisy might have been the one to share that kind of happiness with him, if only he hadn't driven her away. She was like no woman he had ever known. Jake cringed, thinking about his past. Was it possible that he had put all women in the same category? Had he assigned his general mistrust of people to someone who never cared about his money—even if he were to lose it all?

Daisy had already been through so much—the loss of her father, her mother's accident and illness, and now his lie of omission. He had kept her in the dark about what he believed to be true about their parents and hurt her deeply. He couldn't soon forget the crushed look in her eyes. It tore away at him, like a bandage from an open wound. He ached, but he knew this: He wouldn't go after her. She needed something better, someone in her life who wouldn't hide their injuries from the person who could help them heal.

Jake steadied his breathing, hoping that, somehow, sleep would come.

～

DAISY HAD NOT SEEN Jake for two days. She'd noticed a single light on during the evenings, but otherwise, not much sign of life over there. It was for the best, really, though she missed him—despite the lingering anger.

She dipped her paintbrush into a gallon of wood stain and applied it to the balcony railings on her mother's front deck. It felt like months since she had been out here with a sander, preparing these rails for refinishing, but really, it had only been a few weeks. Enough time to spar with an old crush, fall in love, and begin the hard process of picking up the shards of her own heart after that fleeting relationship failed.

She inhaled sea air and refocused on the silvery wood deck. Without Rafael to help her with various tasks, this particular one had dropped low on the list. But she couldn't leave here without smoothing the railing so her mother could, someday, stand out here and enjoy the view.

The crunch of tires onto Jake's driveway pricked Daisy's ears. A car pulled up, stopping only long enough to let out two people and their luggage: a woman and a young girl. Daisy shaded her eyes, trying to make them out. Maggie?

Her heart sank, what was left of it anyway. If Maggie were here for her month at the beach house, that meant Jake might have already moved back to Los Angeles to his work, his phone calls and emails, and his legal problems. She watched the two of them climb up the stairs and knock, a knot forming in her throat.

When Jake didn't answer the door, Daisy put down her brush, pulled off her gloves, and walked across the divide. "Maggie?"

The oldest Holloway sister spun around. "Daisy? Is that you?"

"It's me."

Maggie swept her up in a bear hug, her brunette waves tickling Daisy's face. They hadn't seen each other in years—other than via those video calls—but the gregarious Maggie hadn't changed. Daisy remembered how fun she always was, like a babysitter with chocolate in her purse.

"And this is my daughter, Eva."

The girl was a miniature version of Maggie, with big brown eyes and full hair. "Hi! Are you the Daisy that used-ta live in the house next door? My mom says you were kinda a loner but real nice."

Maggie gasped.

Daisy's brows rose.

"That's not at all what I said." Maggie gave her daughter a chiding look. "I said you played alone a lot, like Eva does—she's an only child too. I did say, though, that you were really nice."

Ah. Okay then.

Daisy glanced at the two suitcases on the porch next to the girls. "Moving in?"

Maggie's smile faltered. "Uh, yes. We're early, though." She slid a glance toward the door. "I haven't been able to reach my brother, but I'm hoping he's here to let me in."

Daisy kept her expression as neutral as possible. She had no idea where Jake was, but couldn't ignore the lift she felt when she learned he might still be around. "I haven't seen him today, but he sometimes goes for a run in the mornings. He usually leaves the back door open."

Maggie sighed, looking relieved. "Perfect. I'm exhausted. We took the train."

"The train? Doesn't that take—"

"About twenty hours."

"Oh my word!" Daisy picked up both suitcases, laughing. "Guess I better help you two with these."

Maggie laughed too. "I just hope he's got a nice coffee maker in there."

"Just you wait. The kitchen is truly beautiful."

As suspected, the back door was open. Jake's expensive running shoes lay on the back porch. Maybe he hadn't gone for a run after all.

Daisy followed the women inside, carrying their bags like a porter. The creak of the hall's old wooden floors greeted them. "I suppose Eva will take this room," Daisy said, stopping in front of the room she had occupied for more than ten days.

Eva ran inside and leaped onto the bed with a lively sigh. "It's perfect!" She sat up and looked at them both. "I'm going to sleep now. Bye." She shooed them away with laughter.

"That was easy," Maggie quipped. "Here, I'll take my bag until Jake gets here. I haven't decided which room will be mine for the month. Will you join me for coffee?"

Daisy hesitated. If Jake suddenly showed up, things could get awkward.

Maggie said, "Please? I need the company."

"Sure. A coffee break would be nice. In fact, let me make it." Daisy led the way down the hall, calling over her shoulder, "I learned my way around here pretty quickly."

Minutes later they each curled up on the couch with a mug of hot coffee, the sky over the beach particularly blue and clear through the picture window. "Colibri really pulled out the best weather for you, didn't it?"

"She really did," Maggie said, looking more relaxed than she did when she first arrived. "I forgot how much I liked it here."

Daisy nodded. "I had the same thought when I came home last month."

Maggie sighed, relaxing a little more. "I'm glad you came over when you did. If you hadn't, we would probably still be out on that porch."

Daisy laughed.

Maggie lowered her voice. "But seriously, I owe you a thank you."

"Me?"

"Yes." Maggie looked at her over her coffee mug. "My brother came clean with me. Told me he had been depositing money into my bank account. Apparently, you're the one who made him fess up."

Daisy let that wash over her.

Maggie set her mug down on the scarred-up coffee table. "You saved my hide, girl. I was giving all the credit to that no-good, deadbeat ex-husband of mine." Her eyes flashed in anger. "And he was lapping it up, taking my praise and never correcting my misperception of him."

"Wow, that's so tough, Maggie. But I'm glad you found out before that went on too long." She held her mug, allowing it to warm her hands. "May I ask … does Eva have a good relationship with him?"

A crease formed between Maggie's eyes. "Not really."

"Oh. Sorry. I didn't mean to pry."

She frowned, her eyes beginning to glisten. "No big deal.

He didn't want to be a father. Broke my heart. He left a long time ago, years ago, really. But he still lurks around sometimes, for what, I don't know."

"That's rough."

"Yeah." She shrugged. "In some ways, coming here was for the best. Finally puts some distance between us."

Daisy nodded, compassion for Jake's sister rising within her. "I'm glad Jake told you how he'd been helping."

"Me too. Not that it makes the heartbreak any easier, you know?"

Daisy did know. She was taking each day as it came, knowing that her mind might heal, but the heart would take longer.

"Here I am talking about my brother being honest with me, and there's something I haven't told him yet. Or anybody." She peered at Daisy. "We were evicted."

Daisy gasped. "I'm sorry." She paused. "Didn't mean to react that way."

Maggie waved at her. "Don't be. It's crazy that I let my debts get me this far into the pit. Even with Jake helping me financially, I still had trouble with my bills. Then my salon closed on me last month." She let out a tortured sigh. "My landlord had enough and kicked us out."

"Oh Maggie." The news battered Daisy's insides, yet she knew that here, Maggie and Eva would be safe. "So, what's next?"

"I don't know, really. We still have several months before we can sell this place. I know I wouldn't be able to pay for the taxes on my own. Hopefully, we'll get a good amount for it."

Daisy nodded, the bad news filtering through her.

Maggie grabbed a pillow and hugged it to her middle. "Enough about me. How about you, Daisy? Your mother doing better now?"

"Yes, much. In fact, I was outside making myself useful when you got here because the home health nurse is there now." Daisy stood. "So good to see you, Maggie. I'll be around for a few weeks more, I think. Maybe we can grab coffee again."

Maggie walked her to the door and gave Daisy a hug. "I'd like that."

Daisy's mind spun with the changes coming to the Holloway house. She turned to go home, when she ran right smack into Jake as he stepped into the house.

INSTINCTIVELY, Jake's hands went to Daisy's waist, the feel of her comforting, sizzling, though mildly awkward. She stiffened, and he immediately put his hands in the air, surrendering.

A familiar voice drew his attention away from the captivating little flower who had met him at the door. "Hey, Jake."

Maggie?

His sister tipped her head, watching him and Daisy, her eyes narrow and assessing.

He stepped toward her. "Maggie? What-what're you doing here?"

She slid a look at Daisy as if the two had been cooking up something. What, he couldn't fathom.

Maggie pulled him into a hug, then slapped him on the back. "Long story, Jakey. But I'm here now and I need a shower." She looked from him to Daisy. "I'll leave you two here to ... chat."

Still stunned by his sister's sudden appearance, Jake watched her bound toward the hallway and out of sight. He sensed Daisy sneaking out the door and stopped her with one swift wrap of his arm around her waist. "Please. Wait."

"I don't think this is a good idea, Jake."

He tipped her face upward with a gentle touch under her chin. "I've been thinking about some things you said, and you were right. You were a distraction for me."

She pushed her arms into his chest and stepped back, but he scooped her closer still until their faces were a breath apart. "One wholly perfect and beautiful distraction. I needed you then, Daisy. And I need you now."

"You're leaving Colibri. Leave me alone to get back to being invisible to you."

He smirked, his eyes heavy. "I'm not that jerk teen anymore."

Daisy lifted her chin on her own now. She looked him in the eyes. "I forgive you for ... not being completely honest with me."

"You were going to say lying. And you'd be right. I lied to you, Daisy, by omission of the facts about what I thought about our parents. I'm sorry."

She nodded, tears visible. He watched her needle her bottom lip and snap a look up at him. "What does any of this matter anyway? Maggie's here and you're leaving soon to go back to your old life away from here. I'll be in Colibri for the foreseeable future. The end of our relationship was inevitable."

He took her hand and pulled her toward the hall. "Come up to the master bedroom. I have something to show you."

Daisy stopped, her face flushed, eyes wide.

Jake laughed. "That's not what I meant."

She exhaled, a confused smile on her face. "Okay."

"Then again," he said, drawing closer, his voice deepening, "I could easily change my mind about that."

Daisy frowned, but he only laughed and pulled her down the hall. "I wouldn't take advantage of you, Daisy. I promise."

He pulled her past a couple of closed bedroom doors, and up the creaky steps to the master bedroom that she'd seen only occasionally. He guided her to sit on the edge of the bed. "Wait here a second." He picked up a leather satchel on a faded credenza, unbuckled the latch, flipped it open, and pulled out a single document.

Jake took a seat next to Daisy on the bed. "First, the good news: We've found Bask."

"The foreman on the hotel project, right?"

"Exactly. The contractor threw him under the bus by spreading the word that Billy messed up. The payoff money ran out and now the guy can't get work anywhere."

"So he's ready to talk."

"Yes. The deposition's tomorrow, in fact."

"That's great news, Jake! So happy for you."

"But that's not the main reason for bringing you up here." He handed her the document. "This is what I wanted to show you."

Daisy's eyes traveled to the page. Her eyes popped open wide and her voice sounded mildly suspicious. "Jake? Is this your, uh, bank statement?"

He tipped her chin toward him until their eyes met. "No more secrets kept, Daisy. None. My father taught me that wild displays of wealth were crude. Not a bad rule to live by, but I went too far. My desire to hide my status almost resulted in my sister going back to the lowlife who had abandoned her and Eva. An unintended consequence."

Daisy continued to hold the bank statement in her hand, stunned. "Shouldn't you be on a list of the richest hunks in the world or something?"

Jake chuckled, grabbed the bank statement from her hands, and tossed it onto the floor. Then he wrestled her onto the bed as she laughed, mockingly fighting him off. He rolled on top of her, their faces inches apart. "Did you just call me a hunk?"

She was laughing now, her wispy blonde hair a hot mess around her. "I might have."

"You really think so?"

Her laughter quieted until all he could hear was the steady rise and fall of her breathing. "Yes," she whispered. "You're the hunkiest guy I've ever fallen in love with."

His smile dimmed, a soberness overtaking him. She loved him. He had no reason to doubt her. And he knew something else: He loved her too.

13

The Following Sunday Night

Jake turned his laptop screen so that all three of them—Maggie, Daisy, and he—could see and be seen. "We're on."

Lacy appeared first. She was sitting on a balcony somewhere, sipping a sunset-colored cocktail. "Don't mind me," she said. "Calling you from work."

Maggie harrumphed at her sister, who was probably doing a site visit of a resort property, something she did often in her sales role. "Must be nice."

Lacy held up her glass. "You know it."

"Hi, y'all!" Bella appeared. She had apparently acquired a southern accent since their last family call.

Grace's face popped onto the screen, her blonde hair in a tight bun, black-rimmed glasses on her nose. She appeared to be typing. "Hi, family." She barely looked up.

"Looks like we're all here," Jake said. He quietly reached over and squeezed Daisy's hand.

Bella's voice rose. "I didn't know you would be there already, Maggie. Did they let you off work early to go out there?"

Maggie exhaled roughly, as if preparing herself for an onslaught of questions. "They let me off forever."

Bella: Oh no!

Lacy: That bites.

Grace: Wait. Did you say something?

Maggie continued. "Long story, but it's all working out now." She slid a glance to Jake. "Lost my job and apartment in the same month, but Jake came to my rescue. He's taking good care of Eva and me."

"Aw, Jakey, you're such a sweetheart," Bella said.

Lacy said, "You sure are, ya big lug."

Grace looked up. "What did you say?"

Maggie's brow furrowed. "Grace Ryan, are you working while on this call? I don't care what big case is going on— this is family time. We need you to pay attention. What's so important that you can't give us one hour of your time on a Sunday night?"

Grace grinned. "Well, if you must know"—she lifted her laptop and turned it toward them all so they could see the photo on it. "I wanted you all to see your new niece or nephew!"

Silence.

Maggie, Jake, and Daisy all lurched forward and stared at the sketchy black and white photo on her screen. "Oh my gosh, Grace," Maggie said. "Are you pregnant?"

Grace nodded, all sign of stress gone from her face. "Yes! The baby's only the size of a sweetpea so far."

Lacy drawled, "I was going to say something about him having a big head."

Bella sighed. "This is the best news, Grace!"

"Tell Chase good job," Jake quipped.

"Aw, that's so sweet, Grace," Daisy said.

"But why the ultrasound so early?" Maggie asked. "Everything okay?"

Grace nodded, still grinning. "We did it to confirm the due date. We have several cases going to trial right around the time the baby's due so—"

"Tell me you did not plan the birth of your baby around a trial date," Maggie said.

"Not exactly." Grace laughed. "But it's helpful to know. That's all."

The room roared with laughter and congratulations.

Maggie waved them all quiet. "Okay, okay. Great news. Let's get caught up on the house now. First, I have to say that the kitchen is absolutely gorgeous. And oh those counters! Jake does amazing work, though he'd never tell you himself."

"Good job, Jake," Bella said.

Maggie continued, "I just filled up the fridge because I'll be cooking all month long. No need to eat out with such a beautiful space to work in. You're all gonna flip when you see it."

"And," she continued, "he updated the master bath quite a bit too."

"But Maggie will have to paint it," Jake said. "I ran out of time for that."

"So how is Colibri Beach so far, Maggie?" Lacy said, cutting in. "Hope you haven't seen No-good Hunter around there."

Jake snorted, remembering the name his sisters had for a guy they all grew up with. Grace mentioned to him that she had run into Luke Hunter when she stayed her month at the house, but he hadn't seen him. Admittedly, Jake doubted if he would have recognized the guy anyway.

Maggie didn't reply, so Jake cut back into the conversation. "I have just one question for you ladies. What did all the hotties call me back then?"

Lacy threw back her head, laughing at that. Bella smiled, and Grace tapped her chin with a pencil. "I believe it was something like Jake the Snake!"

Daisy giggled at this. No doubt she'd had a nickname for him back then, too. He'd have to ask her about that later, when they were alone ...

"Seriously, though, Maggie, how is Eva doing?" Grace asked. "Does she love being at the beach?"

Maggie nodded. "She loves your old room, Grace. Having some trouble getting her out of there, actually, like right now. She wants to lay around all day inside."

"Just like Grace!" Lacy quipped.

Grace rolled her eyes. "Ha ha."

"It's really good to be back, though." Maggie sat back and pulled her legs beneath her on the couch. "I'd forgotten how quirky this old place was. The whole house creaks at night when the wind's roaring, and yet I feel safe here."

They all murmured their agreement.

She turned to Jake. "I do have one question for our brother here, though."

He pursed his lips before saying, "What's that?"

"You guys, this man has so many shoes, more shoes than I've ever seen a guy have. And they're leather and suede. So expensive looking!" She slapped him on the shoulder. "Why all the shoes, dude?"

Bella piped up. "A shoe fetish!"

The rest of the women cracked up, including Daisy, who had seen his penchant for high-end footwear up close and personal.

"Hey," he said, unflustered. "You have your clothes and makeup, and I have my shoes. Leave me alone!"

Maggie laughed heartily at that. "Fine, fine. We all have our weaknesses."

"I hate to be the Scrooge of our happy little family here," Grace said, "but Jake, what's happening with the legal troubles?"

"They're going away. Soon."

"Great. How?"

"The foreman on the project came out of hiding and confessed." He grinned. "They can't pin anything on me now."

A whoop went up, each of his sisters offering congrats and virtual hugs. Lacy leaned in closer to the screen. "Good job, bro."

Now that the call seemed to be winding down with nothing too serious to deal with, Jake figured it was the right time to come clean about something else. "Okay, my turn. I have something to tell you all."

Both of Lacy's brows lifted, her lips puckered. "Wow, again? The guy who hardly says two words on these calls?" She took a sip of her cocktail and settled back against her chair. "This I have to hear."

"I wanted you to know that I'll be featured in a magazine soon. Now you know me, I'm a private guy. This is not something I sought out."

Grace frowned. "But you let them interview you?"

"Yes, but only because they were going to include me in the story whether I wanted them to or not."

Bella, the bookworm of the group, perked up. "What kind of story are they doing, Jake?"

He looked into the screen. "Something about hunks, I believe."

"Oh my gosh." Maggie shook her head, cracking up. "Idiot."

Lacy and Grace laughed, while Bella appeared a bit confused.

"Just kidding." He cracked a smile and slid a quick glance to Daisy. "It's about billionaires under thirty-five."

Lacy dropped her cocktail, the sound of breaking glass reverberating on the call. She didn't flinch. "You know, big brother, they don't put guys into billionaire articles who are not actually, you know, billionaires."

"I know."

The call went quiet, as if they were all processing. He continued, "Look, my company is doing very well."

"Obviously," Lacy said, dryly.

"But my investments put me over the top. I don't expect you to read the article, but I wanted to alert you that it would be out in a couple of months. I wanted you to hear it from me first."

"Wow, Jake," Bella said, finally. "That is a lot of zeroes to process."

Lacy continued to watch him with some suspicion. That bothered him—he would probably have some explaining to do to her. But they had been close in the past, so he felt hopeful she would come around.

Grace cut in to his thoughts. "So Jake, is this one of those bachelor billionaire articles? You aren't planning to go on any dating shows to announce your single status, I hope."

He grinned, widely. "Not a chance. If it was an article like that, I wouldn't have been able to participate."

"Wait a second," Bella said. "You're not single?"

He sent Daisy a wink. "Not anymore."

Amidst all the gasps, Jake turned to Maggie and handed her the key to the house. It was a symbolic gesture, as he had already made her a copy this week. Still, it meant something to publicly pass the baton to the next sibling who would be fulfilling their part of the family bargain.

"Maggie," he said. "I formally pass the Holloway family beach house to you." He cinched Daisy close to him, guaranteeing that all of his sisters could see her on the screen. "Because this billionaire bachelor has a wedding to plan."

Daisy squealed and lifted her left hand, showing off the diamond that Jake had bought her when he'd disappeared last week. Maggie lunged forward and grabbed Daisy's hand, screaming like a crazy woman. "That is the biggest rock I've ever seen!"

The other siblings laughed, calling out their congratulations along with myriad questions, such as:

"Where will you live?"

"When's the big day?"

"Will you be building a mansion somewhere?"

Too many questions to answer at the moment, but he

didn't care. The old living room sounding like one big, happy, and loud party.

While his sisters continued to converse, and question, and carry on with each other, Jake pulled Daisy into his arms. "I can't wait to start something brand new with you, Daisy Mcafee," he whispered. "Keeping the good things from the past and putting the not-so-right behind us."

Daisy gazed up at him, her hands entwined in his. "You're the best thing to ever happen to me, Jake. I mean that."

Jake grinned and sealed their future with a kiss so soft, so wild, that he thought he might not survive it. As his sisters made disgusting kissing noises in the background, he pulled Daisy closer, thankful for the memories past ... and those that were yet to come.

ALSO BY JULIE CAROBINI

Julie's books are available wherever books are sold, including her online shop: JulieCarobini.com

Beach House Romances

Beach Sunrise (book 1)

Beach Memories (book 2)

Beach Secrets (book 3)

Beach Sunset (book 4)

Beach Music (book 5)

Standalone

Reunion in Saltwater Beach

Hollywood by the Sea Novels

Chasing Valentino (book 1)

Finding Stardust (book 2)

Sea Glass Inn Novels

Walking on Sea Glass (book 1)

Runaway Tide (book 2)

Windswept (book 3)

Beneath a Billion Stars (book 4)

A Sea Glass Christmas (book 5)

Otter Bay Novels

Sweet Waters (book 1)

A Shore Thing (book 2)

Fade to Blue (book 3)

The Otter Bay Novel Collection (books 1-3)

The Chocolate Series

Chocolate Beach (book 1)

Truffles by the Sea (book 2)

Mocha Sunrise (book 3)

Cottage Grove Cozy Mysteries

The Christmas Thief (book 1)

The Christmas Killer (book 2)

The Christmas Heist (book 3)

Cottage Grove Mysteries (books 1-3)

ABOUT THE AUTHOR

JULIE CAROBINI is the author of 22+ inspirational beach romances. Her books feature captivating heroines, endearing heroes, and a cast of quirky friends, all bound together by the secrets they keep. Her bestselling titles include *Walking on Sea Glass, Runaway Tide,* and *Reunion in Saltwater Beach.* Julie has received awards for writing and editing from The National League of American Pen Women and ACFW, and she is a double finalist for the ACFW Carol Award. She is the mother of three grown kids and lives on the California coast with her husband, Dan, and their rescue pup, Dancer.

Please visit her at
www.juliecarobini.com

Made in the USA
Las Vegas, NV
15 March 2024

87267774R00111